"Go away,

Brutus sighed, th[...]
kiss before scram[...]

"What? You want [...] happened after you
deserted me last night?" Callie asked the anxious
dog. "I made a fool of myself, that's what
happened. There I sat, on Julian's lap no less,
feeling all strange, when he—"

Brutus growled.

"Not that, you silly thing. Julian's been a
perfect gentleman. I'm the one who's gone off the
deep end—"

Brutus snorted, apparently agreeing with her.

"Give me a break, will you? It's only natural I'd turn
to my . . . my stepbrother in my time of need."

Callie shoved the dog away and glared at him.
"That's a disgusting noise!"

Day Leclaire thanks her husband and her family for being the prod that got her writing initially and kept her writing until she sold her first book to Harlequin. Although her young son constantly devised new and more ingenious methods to distract her from her computer ("I just wanted to see if the smoke detector really worked. Can you play with me now?"), her husband was equally clever at keeping Day slaving away ("I see McDonald's is hiring!").

Of course, after the publication of her first book, Day's own enthusiasm took over.

Books by Day Leclaire

HARLEQUIN ROMANCE
3028—JINXED

WHERE THERE'S A WILL
Day Leclaire

Harlequin Books

TORONTO • NEW YORK • LONDON
AMSTERDAM • PARIS • SYDNEY • HAMBURG
STOCKHOLM • ATHENS • TOKYO • MILAN

ISBN 0-373-03139-4

Harlequin Romance first edition August 1991

To my mother,
HAZEN FAIRBANK TOTTON
for reminding me what a wonderful
character Brutus would make,
and
To my good friend,
RUTH JEAN DALE

WHERE THERE'S A WILL

PROLOGUE

Rule #7:
Your workplace should be like your mind;
Channeled, Harmonious, Adaptable, Organized
and Serious.

AT PRECISELY 7:55 a.m. Julian Lord stepped onto the crosswalk at West Chicago Avenue and North Dearborn Street. At precisely 7:56 Julian lay flat on his back, staring up at the hazy Chicago sky. It took him a total of thirty-three seconds to fully appreciate his predicament and regain his feet. Another seventeen seconds were relentlessly consumed while he searched for his tortoiseshell-rimmed glasses, now minus one lens. A final eleven seconds ticked by while he recovered his black Italian leather hand-tooled briefcase, deep jagged scar provided at no additional cost.

By that time, the taxicab that had come within a whisker of killing him was long gone.

When he arrived on the twenty-first floor of the McMillan building, it was 8:01 a.m. and Julian was one minute and one second late for work—and furious.

"Mr. Lord!" Mrs. Pringle gasped as he thrust open the plate-glass door marked Executive Time Management, Incorporated. "What in the world...?"

"Nothing in or of this world at all, Mrs. Pringle," Julian stated with force. "Chicago cabdrivers have always been products of hell and are bent on sending the rest of us there as speedily as possible. Foiling their latest attempt on my life was due solely to my split-second reflexes and a strong instinct for self-preservation." He straightened his tie and allowed a small grin to ease the corners of his mouth. "It's a relief to discover I didn't lose my edge during my stay in California."

An answering gleam of amusement brightened Mrs. Pringle's eyes. "It is indeed, Mr. Lord. I trust your trip was successful?"

His grin broadened. "Quite successful." He glanced at the pile of correspondence stacked on his secretary's desk and his humor faded, to be replaced by a crisp back-to-business manner. "Let's get started, shall we?"

"Your knee?" she mentioned, glancing at his torn trouser leg. "It's bleeding. Should I—"

"Thanks, but don't bother. I'll take care of it as soon as we're done here. What's the most urgent?"

Mrs. Pringle nodded her acceptance and sighed. "It all is."

Julian didn't say a word, nor did he have to. A single raised eyebrow was all the prompting his secretary needed.

She handed him a number of letters. "These should have immediate responses, Mr. Lord. The rest can wait." She picked up her pencil and notepad, ready to record his instructions.

Julian flipped through the papers. "Schedule the Telemat Company for our time-management course the second week in September, FMT for the week after that." He crumpled a third letter and tossed it with unerring accuracy into her trash basket. "We're wasting our time trying to deal with that gentleman. And as for this other matter..." He thought for a moment, tapping the memo in his hand. "Return Mr. McMill's call and tell him we're interested. Make an appointment for him with Brad."

"Yes, sir. And those final three letters?"

He sifted through them. "Yes to the first one. No to the second and third." He dropped the letters on her desk. "Any phone messages?"

"They're all on your desk, except for this one from your stepsister." His secretary handed him a slip of paper. "She called just after five yesterday."

A frown touched his brow. "Did she say what she wanted?"

"Not exactly. I had a bit of trouble understanding the problem. When I explained that you were already on a plane headed home and couldn't be reached until today, she seemed...somewhat at a loss."

His frown disappeared and he gave an indulgent laugh. "Knowing Callie, I don't doubt that for a moment. I'll give her a ring as soon as I have time to deal with her latest disaster. Is that all you have, Mrs. Pringle?"

"That's it."

"Then please make a list. First. I want to see Brad Anderson. Now. Three minutes ago would have been even better.

"Second. I'll need you and your steno pad in my office in thirty minutes to clear up the rest of this backlog.

"Third. I want a black double-breasted pin-striped suit by either Canali or Geoffrey Beene, and a tailor who knows which end of a needle to thread, up here before the end of the day. You can find my measurements in my personnel file.

"Fourth and final. Contact my ophthalmologist for my prescription and have a new pair of glasses made. I want black frames this time, both functional and businesslike. See to it they're delivered as soon as possible. I think that should do it for now. Any questions?"

Mrs. Pringle jotted down the last of his instructions and looked up, giving him a quick shake of her head. "Not a one, Mr. Lord. I'll take care of this right away."

"Excellent." He shot her a look of approval. "I don't know what I'd do without you."

"Nor do I," Mrs. Pringle concurred.

Julian's lips quirked upward. "Your modesty does you credit, Mrs. Pringle," he informed her gravely. With that, he strode into his office.

Before the door closed behind him, Julian had the balance of his day mentally scheduled. Things at Executive Time Management were about to undergo a drastic change—change that would wreak havoc with his own routine, as well as the routine of his company. It would be quite a challenge to channel the threatening chaos into his own sound and orderly system. He smiled with a hint of satisfaction. He'd always loved a good challenge.

He stepped toward his desk and a slight throbbing in his left leg reminded him of his run-in with the cab. With a grimace, he stared down at the rent in his trousers. It was not a pretty sight.

Crossing to the ensuite bathroom, he opened the medicine cabinet and removed the first-aid box. Taking out the small pair of scissors, he enlarged the ragged tear. Within moments the messy abrasion on his knee was cleaned, dabbed with antiseptic ointment and covered with a gauze bandage.

"My wife couldn't have done it as well," a voice commented from the doorway.

Julian spared his partner a brief glance, then deadpanned, "So get rid of her. I've long believed wives are an overrated commodity. Their function in society is purely ornamental and therefore impractical."

"Oh, I don't know." Brad Anderson leaned against the doorjamb and grinned. "I can think of one or two other uses they serve."

Julian's lips curved into a smile. It was an old game, one they'd shared in boyhood and continued through their school and college years. "The main function of matrimony is the legalized propagation of the human race," Julian said, intoning the required litany. "And since we're already well propagated as it is . . ." He shrugged, allowing the statement to hang, and began to restore the bathroom to its former pristine condition.

Brad's grin broadened. "And the other, er, function they serve?"

"Despite current propaganda, *that* delightful pastime does not require marriage." Stepping past Brad, Julian stripped off his grease-stained jacket and hung it in the closet.

"Poor Julian." His friend shook his head pityingly. "I'm beginning to think you actually believe that garbage we used to spout. Look at you. Thirty, rich, single—and secretly miserable."

Julian's expression held amazement. "I am?"

"You are," Brad confirmed. "But you'll discover the error of your ways soon enough. One of these fine days, you'll snap up a tasty morsel and find a hook in your mouth the size of an anchor. Then some pretty little thing's going to reel you in, fillet you within an inch of your life and serve you up as sushi."

Julian chuckled. "No way. That was your mistake, my friend, not mine. There should be a law against marrying your high-school sweetheart."

"So says the man who had so many high-school sweethearts he couldn't decide which one to choose."

"So I gave them each a fond kiss farewell and sent them on their way—a course of action I strongly recommend." He deliberately changed the subject. "Now, fill me in on what I missed this past week." He headed for his desk and seated himself behind it. "How have Grieg and Sampson worked out? Are they capable of leading some classes on their own?"

"Are they ever! They're incredible finds. We can start sending them out tomorrow, as far as I'm concerned. I have enough lectures booked to keep them busy for the next eighteen months, minimum."

Julian nodded in satisfaction. "Excellent."

"Okay. Okay. Enough with the mundane," Brad said, pacing in front of Julian's desk. "I can't stand it anymore, so spill it. What happened in California?"

"Not much." Julian leaned back in his chair, keeping his expression carefully bland. "We only had the third-largest computer company in the country offer us a package deal. They want to combine our time-management classes with a specially developed computer program to match. You know the concept—a nationwide promo and a huge publicity campaign featuring our classes and their exclusive program." He allowed that to sink in before adding, "There's only one hitch."

Brad sat in the chair in front of Julian's desk, a stunned expression on his face. "I knew it was too good to be true. There had to be a hitch somewhere."

Julian leaned forward. "Wait until you hear it. They want a book to complete our end of the package. They think it would be a surefire bestseller. Can you believe it? We've discussed that very thing ourselves. I've even got most of the preliminary work done. A few months of concentrated effort and we could have it all!"

With a loud whoop, Brad leapt to his feet. "Yes! There'll be no stopping us now."

Julian gave him a few minutes to gloat before bringing him down to earth. "Time to get practical, Brad. This is a fantastic opportunity, no mistake. But we need to act. Now. It'll mean changes and it'll mean a lot of hard work over the next few months."

Brad rolled up his sleeves. "Ready. Hit me."

"First. You'll need to take over my accounts and the operation here. You said Grieg and Sampson are ready, so use them for the fieldwork while you do the pencil pushing."

"We'll need more staff," Brad warned.

"Then take care of it. Second. Coordinate everything through me. I don't want any screwups. Third. I intend to base myself at Willow's End. I'll need peace and quiet while I write this book."

"Aunt Maudie's place for peace and quite? You're kidding. How do you expect to get any work done at Willow's End?"

Julian dismissed his partner's doubts with a smile. "Maudie's brand of confusion doesn't bother me anymore."

Brad snorted. "That's not what you said two months ago. You made me promise to shoot you the next time you talked about visiting again."

"I always say that. But I intend to handle things differently this time," Julian informed him. "After all, management and organization *are* my areas of expertise."

"They were supposed to be your areas of expertise before," his partner pointed out, "for all the good they did you. You know there isn't anyone or anything that can manage Maudie, let alone organize her." Before Julian could argue the point, Brad said, "So tell me what's fourth and final. You *always* have a fourth and final."

Julian relaxed back into the leather curves of his chair and grinned. "Fourth and final. Go out and buy us the biggest most expensive bottle of champagne you can get your hands on."

Brad's eyes gleamed in anticipation. "You've got it!"

"Mr. Lord?" Mrs. Pringle stuck her head into the office, her expression alarmed. "A telegram just arrived for you. It's marked 'Urgent.'"

Julian gained his feet in an instant. Swiftly he crossed to the door and snatched the telegram from his secretary's hand. He tore it open and scanned the contents, the pale yellow pieces of the envelope fluttering heedlessly to the floor.

The color drained from his face and he inhaled sharply. "Oh, God," he muttered, then bit out, "Mrs. Pringle, call the number at Willow's End. See if you can get through to Callie. And please... hurry!"

"Right away, Mr. Lord," Mrs. Pringle whispered, and whisked out of the room.

"Julian, what is it? What happened?" demanded Brad.

"It's Aunt Maudie. Callie says she's gone."

Brad wrinkled his brow. "Gone?" Then understanding dawned. "She's died? Oh, no. Holy Christmas. Julian, I'm so sorry."

A muscle jerked in Julian's jaw. "That makes two of us." He knew his response was stark, but it was impossible for him to say anything else—not when he felt as though the best part of his life had just been ripped away. He crossed to his desk and buzzed the outer office. "What's the holdup, Mrs. Pringle? I need to speak to Callie."

"I'm trying, Mr. Lord, but there's no answer. I'll keep ringing."

"Please do." He yanked his tie loose and sank into his chair. "Not Maudie," he muttered, scanning the telegram once again. "Anyone but Maudie. I can't lose her yet."

"She raised you, didn't she?" Brad offered tentatively. "You were, what... six when your mom died?"

It took a long minute for Julian to answer. Then he nodded, speaking slowly, his voice deep and rough. "Six, and the worst little monster that ever roamed the earth. Dad couldn't be bothered with the hassle of it all. His archaeological digs always took priority. But Maudie had time for me. Maudie always had time. So we moved in with her—or at least I did.''

''What does the telegram say?''

''Not much. At least, not much that I can understand. There's something here about today at 3 p.m. If it's true, if Maudie's... I've got to get out of here. I've got to go home to Willow's End.'' Julian snatched up a pen and began to make a list. ''I want you to take care of these details for me.''

''Sure, Julian. No problem. Whatever you need.''

He tore off a page and started on a second, his pen breaking beneath the pressure of his fingers. Dark blue ink squirted out, spreading across the paper. The words he'd written blurred into a meaningless jumble.

Muttering an expletive he jabbed at the intercom button. ''Damn it, Mrs. Pringle. What's the delay? I need some answers and I need them now!''

CHAPTER ONE

Rule #2:
Time is money.
Which makes every second count.

CALLIE MARCUS sat on a blanket beneath the giant old oak tree in the middle of Miller's Park, her cherry-red skirt spread in a wide circle around her. She ignored the milling crowd gathered for Maudie's memorial service and instead stared down at the scraps of paper littering her lap.

A feeling of dismay crept over her. She'd never sort Maudie's notes in time. Never. And it was so important that she accomplish this first task well.

Maudie had made three requests before she died. The first lay ahead and would prove the most emotional. The second request, finishing the repairs to their home, Willow's End, would take the most work. And the third, helping two youngsters stay out of juvenile hall for the summer, would be the most challenging. But right now she needed to concentrate on the first of the three.

She scooped up a handful of assorted bits of paper, each one a "page" out of Maudie's peculiar idea of a journal. She'd once described the miscellaneous notes as special memories she'd jotted down "marking the kindness of others." They were like snapshots of her life, and Callie, watching as years' worth of captured moments trickled through her fingers, wished for even half so many wonderful events during her own lifetime.

It amazed her how each slip of paper, each separate memory that Maudie Hannigan had recorded and saved in her "memory drawer," connected her great-aunt's life with someone else's in Willow, like a huge patchwork quilt. Lives that touched lives that touched lives.

How do you thank someone for a memory? She tucked a long strand of chestnut-brown hair behind her ear and considered. That had been her great-aunt's first request when she realized her death was imminent—to use the notes she'd saved over the years to thank all the special people who'd been part and parcel of her life. And Callie would do it, too, one way or another. She selected a note at random, her lips curving in a bittersweet smile. At least, she'd do it if she could decipher Maudie's handwriting.

A shadow fell across the paper and Callie looked up, shading her eyes against the bright afternoon sunshine. It didn't surprise her to see her friend, Valerie. Where others might hesitate to approach at such a time, the cheerful brunette didn't think twice about it. "Don't tell me," Callie guessed. "I'm late, right?"

"Just a little," Valerie agreed gently, bouncing her gurgling six-month-old son on her hip. "It's hardly worth mentioning, though." She smiled at the baby, running a loving hand over his coal-black hair. "Hardly worth mentioning at all, is it Danny?"

Well aware of her friend's talent for understatement, Callie couldn't prevent a wry note from entering her voice. "I'm almost afraid to ask, but how much is 'hardly worth mentioning'? My watch broke months ago."

Valerie joined her on the blanket and released the squirming baby, who crawled over to Callie. "There's no rush. It's only twenty past three. People understand, and besides, everyone's enjoying the sunshine."

Callie glanced down at all the notes left to be sorted. Danny made a grab for the bright scraps and she caught his hand. "I'm already late, so a few more minutes won't make much difference, I guess. I should have organized this last night, but I ended up—"

"Helping poor Mrs. Banks with her sick husband instead of taking care of yourself. Yes, I know."

Callie sighed, wishing she didn't feel so helpless, a sensation as uncomfortable as it was uncommon.

Valerie touched her arm. "Are you all right?" she asked compassionately.

"Sure," Callie said, then shook her head. "No. I guess I'm not." Tears blurred her green eyes, and the tightness in her throat made her words soft and husky. "I miss her, Valerie. I miss her so much."

"We all do, honey." Valerie gestured toward the huge crowd gathered in the field. "Every last one of them feels the same way. But they're here for *you,* as much as they are for Maudie."

Callie lowered her head, struggling to control her emotions. She knew Valerie was right. The people of Willow would give her all the support she needed. It was one of the things that made the town so special. It was something in which she'd taken amazed delight when, eleven years ago, her mother, Helene, had married Maudie's nephew, Jonathan Lord.

Callie had been fascinated by all of it: the town of Willow, Maudie, Maudie's huge old house, Willow's End. She'd also been impressed to learn that the house had been in the Hannigans' possession for generations. Maudie and Willow's End were the first stable dependable things Callie had ever known in her life. For a while she'd thought she was in heaven, reveling in both country living and the friendliness of the townspeople.

Unfortunately the marriage between Jonathan and Helene was doomed to failure. Unlike Callie, Helene hated the slower pace her life had taken and found the familiarity of the neighbors intrusive. Bored with both Willow and her most recent husband, Helene filed for divorce after only three years, anxious to move on to a larger city and another husband.

When Helene told her daughter they were leaving, Callie, for the first time in sixteen years, balked at the idea of yet another move—particularly one that would take her away from Maudie and Willow's End. Thanks to Maudie's insistence and Helene's less than motherly attitude, Callie had remained behind, never once regretting her decision.

She looked around at those who'd come to mean so much to her. The warmth and generosity of spirit she'd found in Willow tied her irrevocably to this place, and if she was very lucky, she'd never, ever have to leave it. But to address so many people, to say a final goodbye to Maudie... how could she go through with it?

"Don't fuss over some fancy eulogy," Valerie urged, as if sensing Callie's inner conflict. "It'll only make things that much more difficult." She plucked Danny off the perch he'd found on Callie's leg. "And you know full well no one's going to mind if you don't have your speech all polished and perfected."

That won a grin from Callie. "I'm relieved to hear it, because I don't have a speech at all." She indicated the pile in her lap. "Just Maudie's notes."

Valerie chuckled. "That's even better. You can read us Maudie's words of wisdom and we'll have a laugh together. She'd have wanted that." She tilted her head to one side, sympathy reflected in her dark vibrant eyes. "All right?"

Callie nodded. "Yes, I think so." She scooped up the notes and stood, shaking out the red skirt of her sundress. Looking around at the waiting crowd, she walked to the small podium set in the middle of the field, fighting back the emotions that threatened to choke off her words before they were spoken.

She piled the papers into a heap on the lectern and gazed out at Maudie's friends and neighbors, all of whom had come to pay their final respects to one of Willow's most beloved citizens. They sat on blankets and lawn chairs, or lay sprawled in the long cool grass. Gay beach umbrellas were scattered across the meadow like so many giant colorful butterflies, shading people from the hot June sunshine. And every last person wore brightly hued clothing, just as Maudie had requested.

Callie cleared her throat, forcing herself to ignore both her nervousness and her sorrow. She couldn't indulge in such feelings right now, not when Maudie needed her.

"Thank you all for coming," she began in a clear even voice. "I know Maudie would have been honored by such a tremendous turnout. Celebrating her life here—" she indicated the surrounding park "—in one of her favorite spots, seems only fitting. It also gives me the opportunity to reminisce about the special times many of you shared with her."

There was a faint murmur of voices, and like the comfort of a loving parent, a benevolent warmth reached out to encompass Callie. She shut her eyes for a moment, welcoming the serenity that settled over her. Valerie was right. These people were here for her. Perhaps fulfilling Maudie's first request wouldn't be so difficult, after all. If only the other two proved equally simple.

Callie shuffled the notes together and extracted one at random. She read what was written on it and almost laughed aloud. "Jesse Jacobs." She scanned the crowd, spotting the tanned farmer's bright silver hair. "Seems we've got you to thank for increasing our household by one member—and our more infamous member at that."

Jesse shook his head in mock dismay. "That pup I gave Maudie was supposed to be my thanks to her for nursing my wife through pneumonia six winters ago."

"Thanks or punishment?" a voice called out.

Callie laughed along with the others. "Good question, Nelson. And I might believe you meant it if you hadn't stitched Brutus up after his run-in with that plate-glass window."

"Obviously done before our fine vet got to know what kind of dog Maudie had been given," Mayor Fishbecker pronounced from his seat in front of the podium.

"If Brutus heard you call him a dog," Nelson retorted, "it would take more than a few stitches to save your hide."

"Which makes me eternally grateful he's not here. Had to lock him up, did you, Callie?" The mayor's question elicited knowing chuckles.

She nodded, unable to hide her amusement, though it warred with her feelings of guilt at excluding Brutus from such an important occasion. But, again, she'd been following Maudie's instructions. Which meant that Brutus stayed incarcerated in the house.

"At least we have a place to call home," Callie stated, pulling another note from the pile. "If you hadn't delayed the foreclosure, Mayor, Willow's End would have been auctioned off to redevelopers."

The heavyset mayor mopped his brow, his face ruddy from a combination of sun and embarrassment. "It was those darned property taxes Maudie kept forgetting to pay. Not that she forgot after that. Besides, what else could I do? She made the best danged fudge in the county."

Callie nodded, her voice wobbling ever so slightly. "She did, didn't she?" From the instantaneous response around her, it seemed every person there had had an opportunity to sample—and delight in—Maudie's fudge.

It gave Callie an incredible sense of community spirit, realizing how well these people knew and loved Maudie Hannigan. Callie caught her lip between her teeth. Despite everyone's support, the hurt remained. Each piece of paper she read drove the pain a bit deeper. If only her mother had come. Or Julian.

She surveyed the crowd for the third time that afternoon, searching for her stepbrother's distinctive height and features. Bewilderment mingled with apprehension when she failed to spot him. He must have received her telegram—now that she'd sent it to the right address. He wouldn't stay away because of past...disagreements. Would he?

He'll come, she tried to reassure herself. *You know he'll come—if only because of Maudie.*

"Hey, Callie," six-year-old Simon piped up. "Am I in there?"

With a feeling of relief Callie made a production of checking through her notes. "You sure are. Something about a trout caught with a rope, a safety pin and a cricket?"

Simon grinned proudly. "My very first fish and your aunt Maudie cooked it up for our lunch."

"I remember," Callie said. "She claimed it was the finest trout she'd ever tasted." She pulled out another slip of paper without giving herself time to think or dwell on her loss.

"Speaking of trout, it seems we have the Burns brothers, as well as Simon, to thank for keeping our fish population under control. Some of Maudie's fondest memories were of sneaking out to join your midnight fishing parties." She looked at the three lanky redheads in question. Seeing their identical expressions of horror, she clapped a hand to her mouth. "Oops. Let me guess. It was supposed to be a secret."

"You got that right," the oldest one muttered. "Sure isn't one no more. Not with Pop standing right here."

"And now that he knows your little secret, consider yourself grounded, my boy," their father said.

Callie snatched up another piece of paper. "Josiah Hankum," she read hastily. Her brows drew together in confusion. "I don't quite understand what she's written here. Perhaps it was before I came to Willow. She says, 'Thanks for the apples.'"

The roar of laughter was deafening. Everyone turned to look at the elderly man, who drew himself up, glaring from beneath thick white brows.

"I'm sorry. I must have made a mistake," Callie said, attempting to remedy the situation. But it only seemed to make matters worse. If anything, the laughter grew louder.

Once it was quiet enough for him to speak, Josiah informed her with dignity, "No mistake, my dear." A humorous gleam lit his eyes. "I'm glad to hear she liked my apples. That rapscallion, Julian, took enough of them home."

"Julian?" Callie couldn't conceal her interest.

"That young scamp was the only person to ever best me at my own game. Which is saying something. He was quite a planner, even then. But if Maudie didn't see fit to tell you about it, then it's a story you'll have to get from Julian himself." With that, Josiah sat down again, his back as straight as an oak tree.

This story she'd have to hear, Callie thought, assuming she could get it out of Julian. Assuming Julian ever decided to show up. Where was he?

Here.

It was almost as though he'd said the word aloud, so clearly did it echo in her mind. She caught a sudden movement from the corner of her eye, and then she saw him. Instinctively she knew he'd been standing beneath the huge gnarled crab-apple tree all along, motionless, his black suit blending in with the scabby dark wood of the trunk. Just as she knew his eyes, behind the dark sunglasses, were focused on her.

Julian was here.

Callie couldn't help herself. She grinned. The despair that had gripped her since Maudie's death slipped away. It didn't matter how she and Julian had last parted. It didn't matter that he'd probably never forgiven her for the part she'd played in ruining his relationship with Gwen. It didn't even matter that he'd worn black. He'd come.

The next hour slid by as Callie wended her way through the pile of Maudie's notes. Some brought shrieks of laughter, others moments of thoughtful silence, and still others brought tears. Through it all, no one stirred. They all stayed to the very end, and when she'd read the last bit of paper, they sat motionless for a long moment. Then, one by one, picnic baskets were opened and conversation started again, gaining in volume until the atmosphere had become cheerful, just as Maudie had wanted.

It took a while for Callie to get through the crowd of people who wanted to speak to her—share stories or special memories of Maudie. Patiently she dealt with them all, until the last person drifted away and she was free to approach Julian.

How should she greet him? What should she say—especially considering they hadn't spoken in a year? Not that that was Julian's fault. He must have found it a wee bit difficult communicating with someone who disappeared every time he came for a visit. She'd felt so guilty about causing his breakup with Gwen, she'd found avoidance a convenient solution.

The initial joy she'd felt upon seeing him faded, replaced by an odd feeling of vulnerability. She searched his face, seeking a clue to his inner thoughts, wondering whether he still blamed her for that final incident with Gwen. But if he did retain any of his former anger, he gave no sign.

His features had grown sharper this past year, stronger. The twin lines that sliced from his high chiseled cheekbones to his squared chin cut more deeply into his face. The smiling mouth she'd once thought so very attractive now had a cool firmness.

Even the slight arch of the slashing brows above his dark glasses hinted at a man in control. From the precision of his haircut to the perfection of his somber suit, he was aloof and contained. Yet beneath the surface, Callie knew, lay a wealth of barely leashed power.

Callie struggled to hide her apprehension, wanting to draw comfort from his strength, as she had for so many years. This man was no stranger; he was her brother. He'd always been there when she needed him. She had only to approach him and things would be as they'd always been. But she hesitated to do so.

Apparently Julian felt no such hesitation. Without a word he swept her into his arms, holding her tight against his broad chest, his hand cradling her head to his shoulder. For long moments she clung to him, relieved beyond measure to have a member of her family to turn to, someone who understood and shared her grief.

"Are you all right?" he asked, pulling away to study her upturned face.

"Yes. Yes, I'm fine. Thanks." She forced herself to hold back the threatening tears, knowing that if she broke down now, she'd never be able to stop crying.

"Are you sure?" At her nod, he demanded, "Then explain to me what's going on around here. What is all this?"

She blinked in bewilderment and stepped free of his embrace. "Didn't you receive the telegram? That should have explained everything. It's a celebration for Maudie." She offered him a tentative smile. "I'm so relieved you got here in time."

"I wouldn't have, if you hadn't started twenty-four minutes late. I went to the church. It was empty. In fact, the entire town is deserted."

Her smile felt more natural this time. "Well, of course it is, Julian. Everyone's here."

"So what are they doing *here?*" He pulled off his sunglasses and the full power of his dark-brown eyes swept over her. "Why are you holding the funeral in the park and not at Maudie's church?"

"Because Maudie wanted it here. She wanted a celebration, not a funeral," Callie said as though that was explanation enough.

"A cele—" He broke off and took a deep breath, shaking his head. "Only you and Maudie could dream up having a...a..."

"Celebration," Callie supplied meekly. She'd been uncertain about how Julian would react to Maudie's request. He didn't seem particularly angry. Though if she was honest about it, he didn't seem pleased, either. Perhaps she should try to pacify him just in case. "Julian," she said, "this *is* what Maudie wanted. She left very specific instructions."

He raised a skeptical eyebrow. "In her will?"

Callie shook her head. "No. At least, I don't think it's in there. Although it's possible she added it without my—" At Julian's impatient movement, she hastened to give a more precise answer. "I don't know whether or not it's in the will. Maudie made the request after her heart attack, before...before..." She lowered her head, her voice dropping to a whisper. "Before she died."

Julian's lips tightened and he turned to gaze out across the park. Glancing up at him, Callie saw a series of emotions flicker across his face. She recognized pain and grief…and perhaps regret? So many times during her teen years she'd turned to this man for solace. Now when he needed comfort, she had no idea how to give it to him.

"Julian?"

He ran a hand through his hair, shoving back the wind-ruffled strands. "I'm sorry, Callie. I didn't mean to bark at you. I found out about Maudie just this morning when your telegram arrived. It drove me crazy, not knowing what was going on and not being able to reach you. I called Willow's End but there was no answer."

"Oh, dear," Callie murmured in distress. "Valerie insisted I stay with her these past two days. I tried calling you earlier this week, honestly I did. But you'd moved from the old address. It took me forever to track you down and let you know about Maudie."

"Forgot my company name again, didn't you, sweetheart?" he teased gently.

Her eyes misted over. "Oh, Julian, I'm so sorry."

He pulled her back into his arms and held her close. "Forget it. I'm here now and that's all that matters." He shook his head. "I can't believe she's gone. Tell me what happened."

Callie made a helpless gesture. "It was her heart. They took her straight to the hospital, but there wasn't anything they could do. You would have been proud of her. She made all these lists of things for me to take care of after…after…" Her voice wobbled. "She knew, Julian. She knew she was going to die."

Julian stiffened. "I thought it was instantaneous. I didn't realize—" He broke off, clearly at a loss for words. "I'm sorry I wasn't there," he said gruffly. "I'd have come if I'd known."

"I know you would have." She moved out of his arms and took a quick swipe at her damp cheeks. "By the time

I'd realized you'd moved and hadn't received my first telegram, it was too late. She'd already gone."

His lips quirked upward, some of the tension fading from his face. "Ah, yes. The telegram." He reached into his pocket and pulled out a folded piece of paper. "You must mean this strange jumble of words that defies intelligent comprehension." He handed it to her. "Since you dictated it, perhaps you can explain it."

"Of course, Julian." Callie looked down at the paper and read: "'Where are you? A.M. gone. Will celebrate Fri. 3 p.m. Park. Black out.'" She shrugged in bewilderment. "What didn't you understand?"

"Pick a sentence," he said, amusement coloring his words. He took the telegram from her and scanned it. "'Where are you?' seems plain enough, I suppose. And though I didn't want to believe it, I suspected the meaning behind 'A.M. gone.' Assuming my guess about Maudie was correct, 'Will celebrate Fri. 3 p.m.' did strike me as a trifle callous—"

"That's a terrible thing to say," Callie said reproachfully.

"My thoughts exactly. I found nothing worth celebrating in Maudie's passing. Let's see now, where was I? Ah, yes. We're up to 'Park' and 'Black out.'" He slid his sunglasses back on. "I have to admit those two stumped me completely."

Julian was right about the telegram, Callie acknowledged with a twinge of discomfort; it did lose something in the translation. At the time she'd sent it, she'd thought it made perfect sense. Perhaps it was the way he read it. He rattled the paper and Callie gave a guilty start, realizing he was waiting for an answer. And waiting was not one of Julian's favorite things to do.

Callie sighed. "Oh, dear. I guess it is a bit confusing, isn't it? You see 'Park' meant—"

"I believe I've since managed to figure that one out. Try 'Black out,'" he prompted.

She couldn't meet his eyes, a blush warming her cheeks. "Well you see 'Black out' meant, um…" Callie cleared her throat, her gaze dropping to the top button of his black suit. "'Black out' meant, don't wear black because Maudie wanted everyone to dress in bright colors."

"Right."

"Instead of mourning her death, Maudie wanted us to celebrate her life," Callie attempted to explain. "She requested we gather here and remember the happy times, rather than the sad. Which is why she didn't want anyone wearing—"

"Black," Julian finished for her. "I'm sure it makes perfect sense—to everyone but me. So what's next on the agenda?" he asked, staring at the crowd of people busy with food and conversation. "What are we supposed to do?"

"We're supposed to stay for the picnic. Are you hungry? I have plenty for both of us if you'd care to share it with me." She sensed his hesitation and knew he was about to refuse. "It's expected of us, Julian. I realize I'm probably the last person you want to be with—"

Julian's brows drew together. "Why would you think that?"

Callie twisted her hands. "I know you must still be angry at me about Gwen, but—"

"Gwen?" She could almost see his brain kick into high gear as he considered her words. "You think I'm still angry about that? Whatever for?"

Callie shrugged uneasily. "Because Gwen…"

"Ended up in the lake?"

"Yes." The word was no more than a murmur. Remorse flooded through her at the memory of Julian's perfectly groomed girlfriend tumbling off the dock and into the cold green depths of the lake.

"Is that why you've spent the past year doing your best to avoid me?" he demanded in disbelief. "Because of what happened to Gwen?"

Callie nodded and, to her horror, felt quick tears sting her eyes. She looked down, blinking to help chase them away. "You were so angry," she said in a muffled voice. "Not that I blame you. If it hadn't been for me, you and Gwen would be married by now."

Julian gave a choked laugh. "Heaven forbid!" He touched her shoulder, his hand warm and comforting. "I'm sorry, Callie. I didn't realize you were still worried about it. I never held that incident against you. As far as I'm concerned it's water under the bridge—so to speak."

She smiled uneasily. He didn't know the entire story or he wouldn't say that; nor would he be so understanding, so kind. And yet, she owed him an explanation. "Julian—"

He stopped her before she said anything further. "I didn't mean to come here and give you a hard time. Not today, of all days. I'd love to have a picnic with you. In fact, I'm starving."

She peered up at him uncertainly. "Really?"

"Really. Friends now?"

Her confession could wait for another day, she decided, not wanting to destroy the unexpected accord between them. "Friends," Callie agreed with a grin. She'd missed her stepbrother over the past year. It felt too good having him back to risk losing him again over uncomfortable revelations. Callie slipped her hand in Julian's. "Come on. If you're hungry, I've got just what you need."

She tugged him toward the shade of a broad sycamore. Beneath it was the blanket and picnic basket she'd set aside earlier that afternoon. Kneeling, she threw the basket open, revealing plastic containers, plates and silverware.

"You weren't kidding about there being enough for two," Julian commented. He unbuttoned his jacket and shrugged out of it, lowering himself gingerly to the blanket. "It's been ages since my last picnic."

"You've been busy."

"Too busy." He scanned the park, a faint smile easing the lines beside his mouth. "The difference between Chicago and Willow is amazing. I bet I could name every person here. Remember all the picnics we used to have?"

"One or two of them seem to stick in my mind." Callie laughed. "Like the time we got caught in that thunderstorm. I thought Maudie would skin us alive."

"It was your sixteenth birthday," Julian recalled. "And Helene was away. You were miserable and I thought a picnic would help cheer you up. Instead all I did was bring the wrath of Maudie down on our heads."

"She was a bit ticked off, wasn't she?" Callie offered him a plate. "Like some cookies?"

"Thanks. How long is this . . ." He raised a questioning eyebrow, gesturing around him with a cookie. "This . . ."

"Celebration."

"Right. How long is this celebration to go on?"

Callie shrugged. "Till people are tired and decide to leave." Seeing his frown, she added, "You're welcome to stay as long as you like, but I have to go home to Brutus before it gets too late." She delved into the picnic basket and unearthed a jar, then twisted off the lid. "Brutus wanted to come. In fact, he's not going to be very happy when we get home. But Maudie said absolutely not." She held the jar out to Julian. "Pickled herring?"

He caught her wrist in an iron grip and moved her hand—and the jar—away from his nose. "*Maudie* said?"

"Well, yes. Before she . . . When she told me how to handle the celebration and everything." Not wanting to dwell on such a painful memory, she continued, "but it wouldn't have been a problem bringing Brutus. At least, I'm pretty sure it wouldn't have been. People aren't all that angry with him anymore.''

He studied her with amused suspicion. "I'm almost afraid to ask. *What* aren't people all that angry about anymore?"

Callie shifted uncomfortably, pulling out a plastic container of jalapeño peppers. "Like one?"

"Not in this lifetime," he stated with force.

"No?" she asked, surprised. "They're awfully good. Anyway, I think people have stopped being angry about the picnic last Founder's Day. Brutus acquired a taste for the German malt and got a little... Well, to be perfectly honest..." She hesitated, popping a hot pepper into her mouth.

Julian closed his eyes briefly. "By all means. Let's be honest."

She glanced around and dropped her voice, leaning a little closer to him. "He got flat-out soused," she confided. "You'd be amazed at the amount of damage one person can do on half a keg of beer."

"Especially when that, er, person is a two-hundred-pound Saint Bernard. The imagination boggles."

Her laughter bubbled up, free and easy. "You don't need much imagination at all. The local television station has it on tape. Don't get the wrong idea—the kids all adore Brutus. My kindergarten class loved it when I brought him in. It's the adults who feel...unsettled whenever he's around."

"Imagine that."

"Oh, Julian, be serious. Now that Maudie's gone, you could get custody of him. He's going to be offended if you keep making cracks like that."

He became the stern stranger again, aloof and exacting. "Callie, Brutus is a dog. Just a dog, nothing more. Perhaps it amuses you to pretend otherwise, but I find it annoying, to say the least."

Callie pulled away from him, indignation darkening her eyes. "I'm not pretending, Julian," she protested. "Brutus really does understand what I tell him."

"I seem to remember your saying the same thing about your daffodils," he reminded her, "when I caught you talking to *them*."

Talking to plants was a perfectly normal activity. He just didn't understand. Callie lifted her chin. "It helps them grow," she explained coolly. "You might also remember my flowers were larger than anyone else's in town. And I do know the difference between daffodils and dogs."

Julian chuckled. "I can't tell you how relieved I am to hear that." He gave her nose a tender flick to take some of the sting out of his teasing.

"You can be as skeptical as you like, Julian Lord," she informed him, refusing to be mollified. She folded her arms across her chest. "But it won't change the facts. Brutus does understand people, so don't say I didn't warn you."

"I wouldn't dare," came the dry response. "Not after six years of hearing you sing the same song."

She eyed him in exasperation. "If we can't agree on simple issues like Brutus, how do you expect us to work out the major ones, like Willow's End?"

Julian raised his eyebrows. "How is Willow's End an issue?"

"Didn't I mention it?" She selected another pepper and bit off the tip. "Either you get custody of Brutus and the house. Or I do."

"Ownership. The word is ownership, not custody. And how do you know who inherits Willow's End?"

She waved the pepper in the air. "Maudie told me. Sort of." She wrinkled her nose at him. "No offense, but I hope it's me. Willow's End won't do you much good in Chicago."

"True. Tell you what I'll do. I'm a reasonable man. If I inherit, I'll *give* you the mutt," he offered magnanimously. "As for Willow's End..." He thought about it for a minute. "You're right. Living in Chicago, I can't give the place the time and attention it deserves. If I inherit it, consider it yours for as long as you want it."

"Really?" Callie struggled for the words to thank him, overwhelmed by his benevolence. "I don't know what to say."

"Say yes," he suggested.

"Yes. Yes. Yes! Oh, Julian!" She launched herself into his arms, scattering bright green peppers across the blanket. "You are the kindest most generous man I know. Once we find Maudie's will, everything'll be perfect."

Julian loosened the stranglehold she had on his neck. "Find Maudie's will?" he repeated in a tight voice. His brows lowered. "*Find* the will? What do you mean find it? It's missing?"

She studied his grim expression in bewilderment. "It's not exactly missing. It's—"

"What's this? Only an hour together and you two are already at each other's throats?" Valerie's light voice interposed and she grinned from one to the other. "Sorry. Am I interrupting something?"

CHAPTER TWO

Rule #4:
Planning is the key that unlocks all doors.

"Yes!"

"No!"

Callie frowned at Julian, before greeting her friend. "Your timing is perfect, Valerie," she said warmly.

"Her timing is *not* perfect," Julian contradicted. "She did interrupt something. And I'd like to know what you mean by missing."

Valerie opened her eyes wide. "Oh, dear. Shall I leave?"

"Since you offered—" Julian began.

"Don't be silly!" Callie inserted quickly, giving Julian a none-too-gentle nudge. "He's just teasing. Aren't you, Julian?"

"No."

"I'm relieved to discover some things never change." Valerie chuckled, her dark eyes gleaming with a wicked light. "And hello to you, too, Julian. Quite some suit you've got there. A bit...black, isn't it?"

His mouth eased into a lazy smile. "How nice of you to notice." He eyed Danny. "I guess you decided to keep the little monster, after all. Couldn't even give him away, huh? That's rough."

"Cretin!" Valerie cradled her son protectively against her shoulder. "Just stay away from him. I wouldn't want anything to rub off." She made a point of turning her back on

Julian and winked at Callie. "Do me a favor, will you? Watch Danny for a few minutes? I have a thousand and one things to get done and it's impossible with a baby attached to my hip."

"Sure." Callie reached up to take Danny, cuddling the drooling baby in her arms. He grabbed at her nose with a wet hand and she chuckled, tickling his tummy until he let go.

Julian raised an eyebrow. "That may not be the most disgusting thing I've ever seen, but it's darned close. Can't you control that son of yours, Val?"

"He's only a baby," Valerie protested indignantly. "Callie doesn't mind. Do you?" She looked at her friend for confirmation, continuing before Callie could respond, "Is it all right if people stop by and pay their respects? They wanted to give you two some time alone, but you've had enough of that, haven't you? The way you squabble, you'd think you were real brother and sister. Oh, I almost forget to ask you, Callie," she added, never once drawing breath. "Mrs. Ashmore wanted to know if you're still willing to bake those cakes for the school fund-raiser and the mayor needs another body on his Save the Belfry committee. I said yes to everybody for you. All right?"

Callie nodded, long accustomed to Valerie and her ways. "Yes, yes and yes. Don't worry about a thing. I've got it covered." She put Danny on the blanket beside her, offering him a rice cake from the picnic basket.

"In that case, I'll see you later," Valerie promised. With a quick flick of her fingers, she hurried away.

Julian watched her go, a pensive expression on his face. "What's with all the favors? Are you doing penance or something?"

She gave him a questioning look. "What do you mean?"

"All these projects. Valerie dumps her kid on you, and then has you sitting on a committee only Mayor Fishbecker could dream up. On top of all that, she's got you baking fund-raiser cakes. If you ask me, it's damned presumptuous, especially considering...recent circumstances.''

"I didn't ask you," Callie pointed out. "And presumptuous? Valerie doesn't know the meaning of the word."

"Get her to look it up sometime."

"You can't believe how supportive she's been the past few days." Callie could see that cut no ice with him. "Besides," she added, determined to make him understand, "I like helping worthy causes."

"Save the Belfry is a worthy cause?" Julian asked in a dry voice.

"Yes, it is," she said with more assurance than knowledge. "As for Danny. I've been baby-sitting him since he was two weeks old and will probably continue to baby-sit him until he gets married."

"Well, before you marry him off, would you mind taking that bug out of his mouth?"

She looked down at the grinning baby and scooped him back into her arms, peering into his mouth. Any bug that might have found its way in there was long gone now. "He probably thought it was a raisin," she said after a moment. "Don't say anything to disillusion him, Julian."

He raised an eyebrow. "Yeah, a raisin with legs. I've got news for you. Unless a certain television commercial came to life in the last two minutes, that isn't what junior just ate. And don't tell me protein is protein."

Callie laughed. "You took the words right out of my mouth." She flicked an ant away from the picnic basket, ignoring Danny's shriek of protest at the loss of a potentially tasty morsel.

"Later, pet. You'll upset your Uncle Julian if you keep this up." She turned to her stepbrother, hoping to distract his attention from Danny's questionable culinary preferences and from any further comments about her volunteer work. "By the way, Josiah Hankum said to get the apple story from you."

For a minute she didn't think it would work. Then Julian nodded, going along with the change of topic. "So I heard."

"Well? Will you tell me about it?"

He rubbed a hand over his hard flat middle. "Only if you feed me. I'm starving. And no more pickled herring."

With an effort, Callie tore her gaze away from the hypnotic play of his long slender fingers. She reached into the picnic basket for another tin, unwilling to acknowledge the strange frisson of awareness that caused her to fumble as she attempted to open the can. After all, Julian was her brother—at least that was the role he'd played for the past eleven years. People didn't get strange tingles over their brother. Or if they did, they shouldn't.

"Here," she offered generously, holding out the tin. "Have a sardine. Now will you tell me the apple story?"

Julian examined the oily tidbit dubiously, then swatted at a fly that found the sardine far more appetizing than he did. "You have a thing for fish, don't you?" he asked, his mouth pulled down in distaste.

She regarded him in surprise. "Doesn't everyone? So, will you tell me about Josiah's apples?"

He shook his head, refusing to give in. "Sardines don't rate the apple story. And don't try that poor-little-me look, green eyes. I haven't bought into it for years."

"Please?"

"I just might be open to a bribe. Tell me you have more in that basket than fish and rice cakes and I'll tell you the apple story. Otherwise, I'm likely to starve before I get halfway through."

"I have more in my basket than fish and rice cakes," she repeated obediently. "Now will you tell me the story?"

He shrugged. "Okay, okay, but it's no big deal." He began to roll the sleeves of his crisp white shirt up past his elbows, exposing the golden-brown skin of his forearms. "When I was somewhere around ten, I heard Aunt Maudie say that Josiah Hankum's apples were the best pie apples in the county."

"So you stole some."

"Wrong," he rapped out, his tone quelling. "School-teachers should know better than to interrupt when others are speaking. Now listen and learn." He returned to his story. "I suppose I could simply have stolen them, but you know Maudie—she'd never approve of that. She'd have made me give them back."

Callie pried open Danny's hand and released the grasshopper he'd captured, wondering whether they grew their limbs back the way starfish did. If not, Mr. Grasshopper was going to have a little trouble living up to his name. "So what clever little scam did you come up with to get Josiah's apples?"

"Old Hankum hated people trespassing on his property. He also hated kids." He frowned at an angelically beaming Danny. "I'm beginning to understand why."

"Julian!"

"Listen, anyone who dines on bugs..." He held up his hands to still her interruption. "Do you want to hear this story or not? Anyway, Hankum especially hated kids who trespassed. And he had a very effective way of discouraging us."

"Which was?"

"You haven't guessed?"

Callie began to laugh. "Throwing apples at you."

"Got it in one. Whenever Aunt Maudie needed apples for a pie, I'd hare on over to the Hankum farm and wait for old Josiah to come tearing out and pelt me with apples."

"Didn't he ever catch on?"

Julian leaned back against the sycamore trunk and gave her one of his slow teasing smiles. "If not, then he was the only one in all of Willow who didn't." He glanced at Danny and groaned in disgust. "Callie, that kid's decided on dirt for his dessert. Can't you control him? No wonder Valerie was in such a hurry to cut out."

She grabbed the picnic basket and pulled out another napkin, applying it to Danny's dirty fingers and mouth. "Are you thirsty?" she asked Julian. "There's lemonade."

"And chocolate-chip cookies. Good as they are, I'd like something more substantial. Do you have anything that's actually *edible* in that basket?"

"How about tofu? No? I have salad," she offered.

"Salad? That's lettuce, right? I can handle lettuce. You did make it with lettuce?"

She popped off the lid and examined the contents. "Nope. Mustard greens and tomatoes with black-pepper dressing."

"No lettuce. And let's take a wild guess here—the dressing is nice and spicy. Right?"

She lifted her brows in disdain. "Well, Julian, if you weren't so particular..."

"Or if you had packed any real food." He reached down and picked up Danny, who was busy gumming at his shoe. "Why don't we just skip the eating part. As pleasant as this has been, we need to get back to our discussion about the disposition of Willow's End. You remember the conversation, don't you? It was right before kid dynamo here dropped into our lives. I believe I left off with '*Find* the will—you mean it's missing?' And you left off—"

"It's not exactly missing," Callie supplied helpfully. "How long can you stay? This might take a while."

"Fortunately for us, I have a while." Julian gave Danny an experimental bounce on his knee. "I was about to invite myself to Willow's End for the summer to write a time-management book, when I heard about Maudie.''

"You were? That's perfect. That would give us plenty of time to work out our little problem."

"Little problem?" Julian questioned. "That's what I've always loved about you, Callie. Your unswerving optimism in the face of overwhelming disaster." He smiled at the face she made and reached for a rice cake, handing it to the greedy baby. "I think I'd better speak to Maudie's lawyer as soon as possible and get a handle on how we should proceed with all this."

"If you think it would help. Though I doubt he can tell us where she hid it."

A long silence stretched between them. "Maudie *hid* the will?" Julian said very carefully, putting Danny down on the blanket. "You didn't mention anything about its being hidden. I know you didn't. You said missing. Now it's *hidden?*"

She frowned at him. "Don't worry, Julian. It's not all that urgent. I already told you what the will says—more or less. We only need to find it in order to verify things legally."

Julian appeared to be struggling with his breathing. "Callie," he managed to get out, "it's not that simple. The court is not going to accept your word alone on how the estate should be settled. Especially when you don't know what her will actually says. They need proof. They need it in black and white. What about Maudie's lawyer? Doesn't he have a copy?"

"Oh, I wouldn't think so."

"Why not?"

Callie hesitated, then reached into the pocket of her skirt and pulled out a pink rose-scented envelope. "Because of this."

He took it from her and turned it over, studying their two names scrawled on the front. "What is it?"

"It's a note to us from Maudie." Callie bit down on her lip. "I found it in the study. It explains about the will and that she hid it."

"I don't believe this. Does Maudie happen to mention where she put her will?"

Callie shot him a look of reproof. "Of course she does."

"Well that's a relief. Where?"

"She said she put it someplace in the house."

"Someplace in the—" Julian ran a hand through his crisp dark hair, the muscles in his jaw clenching. "Callie, that house has three stories, if you include the attic, with two wings and more cubbyholes than a rat's palace. I won't bother to mention the basement, various porches and the vast assortment of storage closets. I don't suppose you could be more specific about where in the house her will might be?"

"No. I can't. That would defeat the whole object of the exercise, don't you think?"

He closed his eyes briefly. "Okay. I'll ask. I'll regret it, I know, but I'll ask. What exercise, Callie?"

She sighed in exasperation. "If you'd read the note, you'd understand."

"Fine." Without another word, he extracted the single sheet of paper from the envelope, scanning it swiftly. "She says I work too hard. What does she mean I work too hard? I do not work too hard!"

"Yes, you do, Julian. She thinks looking for the will would give you a much needed vacation. It'd get you away from all those rules and regulations and . . . and schedules and things."

"What about all your projects and committees? Isn't she worried that *you're* overdoing things. That *you'll* wear yourself out?"

"She doesn't mention it," Callie said smugly. "Her note is perfectly clear, Julian. If we want to find out who inherits the house, we have to find her will. In order to find her will, we have to search for it. Her reasons for hiding it may be a little vague, but think of the good a treasure hunt will do you. It'll be fun. It'll help you relax."

"I am relaxed!"

"Of course you are," Callie said soothingly. "That's why your muscles are all bunched up like that. They're relaxing."

"So I like tension. Sue me."

"Honestly, Julian." Callie shook her head in amusement and glanced down at Danny. He sat quite happily, one hand holding the pickled-herring jar, the other stuffed through the small opening, squishing the bits of fish between his fingers. She extricated his hand and held the jar out. "Are you sure you won't eat something before I pack it all away?"

"No! I want to settle this business about the will!"

"You don't need to shout, Julian," she informed him in her best schoolteacher's voice. "I'm sure it's not healthy for you to turn all red like that. As for the will, there's nothing *to* settle, remember? We have to find it first."

She heard him grind his teeth. "Are you sure you aren't hungry?" she asked, her brow furrowed in concern. "You're looking very strange. Here. This should make you feel better." She reached into the basket and pulled out a small platter, holding it out to him. "Have some sushi."

THE SUN SAT LOW in the sky when Callie and Julian returned to Willow's End. Julian dropped his load of picnic paraphernalia on the front porch and turned back to look at Callie, who stood on the walkway, motionless.

"You coming?" he asked.

"In a minute. I just wanted to look at the house."

"Has it changed?" He came back down the stairs to join her and stared up at Willow's End. "Nope. Still the same old place. And a darned special one, at that." He frowned. "Though now that I look at it, it could use a coat of paint or two. And those shutters are sagging a bit—"

"Don't be so pragmatic. It's a wonderful, beautiful, terrific—"

"And locked house." Julian smiled at her and held out his hand. "I tried the front door. It's locked. Give me the key, will you?" She hesitated and Julian snapped his fingers. "The key, green eyes. Wake up. It's been a long day and I'd like to end it."

Callie shifted from one foot to the other, not quite meeting his gaze. He wasn't going to like this, but there wasn't much she could do about it. "Well, you see, that's the problem. I don't have the key."

"No key? Who has it?" He frowned. "Not Maudie?"

"No. Not Maudie." She cleared her throat. "Actually no one has it."

"No one," he repeated. "No one? You locked the door and no one has the key?"

"You know we never lock doors around here," she told him. "At least we didn't until today. So if there ever was a key, it's long gone now."

Julian closed his eyes, marshaling his thoughts. "What made it so imperative that you lock the door this time?"

"Because of Brutus, of course. I didn't want him to get out."

"Not this again," he muttered beneath his breath. "Callie, listen to what I am about to say and, please, try to remember it. Brutus is a dog. A dumb animal. A creature with a brain the size of a pea and with as much intelligence as your common everyday fungus. He does not have human feelings. He does not have human *anything*. Nor can he open closed doors."

"Yes, he can."

He thought for a moment, then smiled kindly. "Okay. Let's pretend I buy the premise that Brutus can open doors. If he could—which he can't—but if he could, then why didn't you simply chain him up? That way you wouldn't have to lock a door you can't open."

She gasped and drew herself up to her full five foot three inches. "*Chain* him? Chain Brutus? How could you think of such a thing? Do you realize how inhumane that would be? How cruel? He'd never forgive me. Never."

"So he'd never forgive you. I think he's going to be a darned sight less forgiving when we can't get into the house and he ends up starving to death. Or didn't that occur to you?"

Callie struggled to ignore his sarcasm, hanging on to her dignity through sheer willpower. "For your information, I left a window open. All we have to do is climb in and go around and unlock the door from the inside. It's very simple."

His eyes closed again. "I don't believe this. You mean, you lock all the doors because that mutt can open them, but windows are all right to leave open because he can't climb out through those?"

"Well, yes, he can. But he won't."

"God give me strength. Please, I really want to know. Why won't Brutus climb out the window? Does it involve some sort of special doggy honor—thou shalt not escape out windows, but if thou getest open the door, thou mayest?"

Her reply was saccharine sweet. "I want you to know something, brother dear. I hate you. I'm not angry with you, but I've come to realize that I honestly sincerely hate you."

"Thanks."

"Don't mention it."

"You still haven't explained about the window, Callie."

The man was impossible. Why were they dwelling on details when they could be breaking into the house?

"Ever since Brutus skidded through that sliding glass door, he's been terrified of all glass, including windows," she explained. "And I'll tell you something, Julian. I'll regret to my dying day that Gwen got pushed into the lake."

If Julian found it difficult following the progression of the conversation, he didn't show it. "You're sorry she was—"

"Pushed in. Yes. I've spent the better part of last year feeling guilty about it. Now I realize why. You two were made for each other. She was just as precise and perfect as you."

"Thank you again," Julian said, not quite suppressing a smile. "Regardless of what you may have thought, I never held that lake incident against you."

"You deserved each other," Callie continued, ignoring his interruption. "Why Brutus didn't understand that, I'll never know. For some reason he thought you two—"

"Callie!"

"What?"

"Where's the window?"

"Around back. Why? What's wrong?"

"Not a thing, if we stop the conversation now before you say something I'll regret." He walked down the steps and headed around the side of the house, speaking as he went. "I always forget that coming back here is like stepping into an episode of *Twilight Zone*. I'll have to remember to write that down. You tend to retain things better when you record them."

Callie trailed along behind him, determined to be understanding. After all, Julian wasn't acting like himself. Reaction to Maudie's death must have set in, and humoring him seemed the best option. He just needed a long cool shower and a hot dog or more cookies or something. Once she got inside, she'd open a bag of Oreos.

Besides, she shouldn't have mentioned Gwen in the first place. His former girlfriend was clearly a taboo topic. And Callie couldn't blame him for that. If she were honest, she'd admit the incident the previous summer would never have occurred if she'd been more willing to get along with Gwen. So the woman's personality had a few flaws—or more than a few flaws. Personality wasn't everything. It would have taken a bit of work, Callie admitted, but she could have found *something* positive about dear Gwen. Julian had. Too bad it was such a struggle to figure out what.

Julian stopped so abruptly Callie almost ran him down. He stared in disbelief at a narrow window situated just above shoulder height. "That's it? That's the window I'm supposed to crawl through?"

"No," she replied, remembering just in time to humor him. "That's the window *I'm* supposed to crawl through. Even if you could fit in there, you've still forgotten one small detail."

"Which is?"

"Brutus is on the other side."

"So?"

So much for humoring him. "I have no doubt Brutus heard every cruel nasty remark you made out on the front porch. And even if he didn't, Aunt Maudie told me what happened when you visited last winter. I can guarantee you Brutus hasn't forgiven you for that."

"What are you going on about now?"

She put her hands on her hips and spoke sternly. "The firecrackers you set off last New Year's Eve while I was in Chicago chaperoning our sixth-grade field trip. You know how frightened Brutus is of loud noises. He was very upset."

"He was upset? *He* was upset! Did Maudie tell you what he did to my bed? Did she?"

She felt the color burn her cheeks. "He was asleep on top of it when you set the silly things off. He couldn't help it. It was an accident."

"It was deliberate. You know it and I know it."

"Do I?" She opened her eyes wide. "How could it have been deliberate? A creature with a brain the size of a pea and the intelligence of your common everyday fungus committing such a despicable act *deliberately?*"

He took a deep breath. "How do we get in the house, Callie?"

"You're supposed to lift me up to the window and I'll climb in."

He studied the window, then her, and shook his head. "I don't know. In that dress…looks chancy." A wicked gleam glittered in his dark eyes. "I don't suppose you'd care to make a small wager about whether you can get in without ripping something, would you?"

"I don't make bets anymore, Julian," she answered primly. "I haven't for ages."

Julian grinned. "One year does not an age make, sister dear. Which is how long it's been since our last wager. And the only reason you won't bet is because you always lose. Don't you want to try and get even? Bet you a nickel you can't do it."

She pretended to look shocked. "I'm surprised at you, Julian. You realize, don't you, that this is a very serious character defect on your part. You should have outgrown it long ago. Betting isn't logical. It's not good business. It's not *like* you," she informed him. "But make it a quarter and you're on."

"Done."

She stood between him and the house, her hands on her hips. "So? What are you waiting for? Do you want to get in or not? If so, then hoist me up there."

The sun had dipped below the horizon and the shadows grew steadily deeper. The air seemed filled with a chorus of high-pitched chirps and whirs from the many different insects, the deep bass thrumming of a bullfrog setting the beat. An evening breeze blew warm, almost sultry, stirring the chestnut-brown curls of her hair about her neck and shoulders.

In the darkness, she could just make out the white glimmer of Julian's smile. "Let me get this window open a little more and then I'll hoist away."

He leaned toward her, and Callie could smell his crisp light cologne. She stared up at him, unable to move, fascinated by the way the first gentle rays of moonlight etched his face into hard uncompromising lines. Julian seemed so...so different.

He reached past her to brace one arm against the house and lifted the other to open the window further. She should have moved when she had the chance, Callie realized, squeezing out of his way and up against the rough clapboard siding of the house.

The front of his shirt brushed across the front of her sundress and she caught her breath at the unexpected sensation. *What an odd reaction,* she thought, only to feel an even stranger reaction as his strong firm hands closed around her waist.

"Hold on to my shoulders," he instructed, apparently as unaffected by her proximity as she was affected by his. "Dresses aren't made for climbing in windows. But if you sit on the sill and slip your legs through you should remain decent enough. And don't worry, I'll be here to catch you if you lose your balance."

She did as he ordered, laying her hands on the broad expanse of his shoulders, the warmth of his skin burning her palms even through his shirt. She frowned in confusion. This was only Julian. For the past eleven years, he'd been her brother, nothing more.

And he was still her brother, she told herself. Yet she couldn't quite suppress the realization that they weren't truly related.

"Callie, you're going to have to help a little. If you cling any harder, they'll need a crowbar to get us apart."

"Sorry," she muttered. She forced her fingers to loosen their death grip on him and pulled back.

"Ready?" At her nod, his grip on her waist tightened and he lifted her, propping her on the edge of the windowsill. "You all right?"

"Yes." She cursed the breathless quality of her voice, but she couldn't help it. She could feel his chest, firm and broad, pressed against her legs. His arms slid from her waist to rest protectively on either side of her thighs. For one insane instant she was tempted, horribly tempted, to lean forward and allow her body to tumble into his arms.

"Callie?"

She swallowed. "Yes?"

"I'm sure the view from up there is very pleasant. And I certainly wouldn't want to interrupt anything. But *move it!*"

A bucket of cold water in the face couldn't have caused her to react any faster. Callie ducked her head beneath the raised window, and slipped her legs over the sill and into the house, her skirt catching on a splinter of wood. The sound of ripping resounded in the warm night air.

A deep chuckle floated up. "I told you so," he called. "That will be twenty-five cents."

She considered slamming the window and leaving Julian locked outside for the night. But knowing him, he'd find some reasonable solution to his predicament and get in, anyway. Julian was very results-oriented. "So what else is new?" she muttered, then hastened from the bathroom into the main hallway, flipping on lights as she went.

"Brutus?" she called out.

With a light snuffling sound and a funny little groan, Brutus lumbered into view. She hurried to him and sank to her knees. Shoving his ornamental brandy cask out of her way, she wrapped her arms around his massive neck.

"Hello, sweetheart," she whispered into his floppy ear. She traced the stripe of white hair that ran down the center of his head. "You poor thing. Has it been horrid for you stuck here all alone?"

He whined a reply, and buried his face against her shoulder, his breath warm and gusty on her skin. His tail thumped noisily as he flipped it back and forth, hitting the hallway walls.

For a long while they sat there, Brutus "talking" to her with light sighs and tiny yips and Callie responding, telling him every detail she could recall of Maudie's memorial service. Suddenly a loud prolonged banging rattled the house, reminding her of Julian's presence. With a little gasp, Callie jumped to her feet.

Brutus barked in protest.

"Don't say it," she ordered. "I know you're not happy with him right now, but he has reason to be a wee bit annoyed at you, too."

With a snort, Brutus turned his head away.

The noise coming from the front door let her know that if she didn't get there soon, they'd need a new door. "I'm coming!" She gave Brutus a final look of warning, a wasted effort since he continued to sit with his back to her.

"Callie! Open this door! If you don't open up right now—" She unlocked the door and swung it wide. He stood on the doorstep, glaring down at her, his dark eyes burning with fury. "What the hell kept you? No, don't tell me. Let me guess. That stupid mutt. You two got all wrapped up in chatting about your day and forgot you'd left me locked outside."

"Well, yes," she admitted.

"Move." When she continued to stand, staring at him blankly, he repeated his command, his voice firm and final. "Move. Keep your distance and move out of my way. First, I want you to clear a path of all living objects from this door to my bedroom or I won't be responsible for what happens to them. Second. When the pizza man arrives, just send him on up. I'll take care of the tip myself. Third—"

"Julian—" She broke off at his expression and backed out of the way.

He took one step across the threshold and stopped dead, staring in disbelief.

Huge holes had been punched in the hallway walls, wires hanging from the gaping wounds like confetti. Black spray-painted lines and arrows marred what remained of the plaster, and in one corner of the floor, someone had pried up several of the oak boards. A fine layer of gray dust covered everything. Julian looked around in horror, then walked to the nearest door and flung it open.

"Lord, Callie," he muttered. "No wonder you took so long letting me in. Have you called the cops yet?"

"What?"

He grabbed her arm, backing toward the front door. "Come on. Get behind me. We're getting out of here. They could still be in the house."

"Who?"

"Who? The people who trashed this place, of course. Come on! Call that hellhound if you won't leave without him, but we're going. Now."

She resisted his attempt to hustle her out of the house. "Oh. You must mean the redecorating. I know it looks a trifle messy, but it always does when you first pull it apart. Once we get the walls back up—"

"That's not funny," Julian bit out.

Callie blinked in surprise. "It wasn't meant to be. You haven't seen the study yet. How do you think I found Maudie's note? Once we get the walls back up and the plaster hauled away, it'll be gorgeous. Honest."

Words temporarily failed him. "*This* is deliberate? How could you? The home I grew up in, the house I love—" He glared at her. "The house I love with its walls *on*. The house that's been in my family for nearly one hundred years, you did . . . *this* to it? On purpose?"

She tried not to look as insulted as she felt. "Well, of course. Maudie said—"

"Move."

"What?"

"Move. Keep your distance and move out of my way. First. I want you to clear a path of all living objects from this doorway to what's left of my bedroom or I won't be responsible for what happens to them. Second. When the liquor-store man arrives, just send him on up. I'll take care of the tip myself. Third. Don't tempt me to tell you what's fourth and final."

CHAPTER THREE

Rule #11:
*A list is the ladder you use
to reach your goal.*

LATER THAT NIGHT Callie crept along the front walk, pausing halfway to the door to stare up at Willow's End. Every night for the past few nights she'd done the exact same thing. She'd come out to look at the house—to make sure nothing had changed. Tonight, returning from a clandestine visit to the cemetery, she was finally convinced.

The huge old house glowed softly in the moonlight, giving off a warm welcoming feeling. It should seem different now, empty and sad without Maudie. But it didn't. It still gave Callie the same message it had eleven years ago when she'd first arrived there: *Come in, you'll be loved here, I'll protect you.*

She wrapped her arms about her waist and sighed, a tiny smile curving her lips. She'd been so afraid that without Maudie she'd find the soul missing from the house, like a light switched off. But that special inner life was still there. She still had her home.

Beside her, Brutus growled a complaint. "All right, come on then," she said. "Just keep quiet. Those nails of yours are enough to wake the—" He barked his indignation and Callie broke off. "Sorry. I wasn't thinking. But if Julian catches us he's going to want an explanation. Personally,

I'd have a bit of trouble coming up with one. And so would you."

Brutus signaled his annoyance with another bark and Callie put a restraining hand on his muzzle. "Please, Brutus, not so loud. You'll wake him up." She hesitated by the front door, her hand on the knob, and listened. The vibrant trilling of the insect population, which had seemed so romantic before was positively deafening now. How could she hear anything over all that racket?

Taking a deep breath, Callie twisted the handle and pushed open the door. She stuck her head inside and peeked around. "Okay, it's all clear," she called to Brutus. "You can come in."

His instant obedience was as unexpected as it was unwelcome. Not waiting for her to move, he plowed into her, his huge head hitting her square in the middle of the back. Callie went sprawling across the doorstep while Brutus, with an excited yelp, charged into the house. In his eagerness to gain entry he stumbled over her legs and crashed down onto the parquet flooring next to her.

A light came on.

Callie lifted her head, staring at the row of ten naked toes lined up mere inches from her nose. Her gaze moved upward over two large feet followed by a long pair of legs encased in gray sweatpants. Next came a bare broad chest, tanned to an attractive shade of teak, a nicely sculpted neck, and last of all a head and face. The face looked particularly grim.

"Darn."

"Mild, but accurate," Julian concurred. "Too bad. I was convinced this time it really was a burglar. So I brought this with me." He hefted a baseball bat.

One look at the bat and Brutus took off at a dead run. He skidded on the dusty wood flooring, spun in a circle and slammed against the wall at the end of the hall. It took three scrambling attempts before he managed to get around the corner and out of sight.

"Traitor," Callie shouted after him. She sat up and shoved her hair out of her eyes, before looking at Julian. "As much as I love him, Brutus is a flat-out coward. And you take advantage of that. In fact, you always have."

"Me? All I did was come down here to do battle with a thief. How was I to know it wasn't a thief at all, but my own dear sister, sneaking in after a wild night of illicit whatevers."

"I am not your sister," she informed him—a fact she'd only recently determined. "When my mother divorced your father you and I were also divorced. We're...we're ex'es. And I did *not* have a wild night of illicit whatevers."

His lips twitched in amusement. "Then where were you?"

She continued to sit on the floor, pulling her knees up to her chest protectively and wrapping her arms around them. "I...I took Brutus to the cemetery."

Julian frowned. "Callie, it's past one in the morning. What in the world were you doing there at this hour?"

"I know it's late, but I couldn't go any other time." She dropped her chin to her knees. "You see, they don't allow pets at the cemetery. And they don't seem to understand that Brutus isn't a pet. The only way he could visit was if I snuck him in at night."

Julian shook his head in disbelief. "You mean to tell me you broke into the cemetery so that overgrown flea trap could...what? Visit Maudie?"

"Well, yes. No. Not exactly. You see, the women from Maudie's church circle arranged to have a marker erected in her memory, and Brutus wanted to see it."

Julian took a practice swing with the bat. "Brutus told you that, did he? The mutt gets more talented every day."

Callie buried her face in the black denim covering her knees, his sarcasm more than she could handle right then. The tears welled in her eyes and she fought to keep them back. It was late and she was near the end of her rope. She'd used every spare bit of energy in her possession to get through the past few days. She'd tried the best she knew how to do what she thought Maudie had wanted. But she was exhausted, certainly too exhausted to spar with Julian.

The bat hit the floor with a noisy clatter and he swore beneath his breath. "Hey, sweetheart, I'm sorry. I didn't mean to make you cry." He knelt at her side and his strong arms encircled her shoulders.

"I'm not crying," she denied in a husky whisper as a solitary tear slid down her cheek.

"So I see." There was the merest hint of gentle humor in his voice. "Come on. Tell your big brother all about it."

"You keep forgetting," she managed to choke out. "You're not my brother anymore."

"If that's what you want, it's fine by me. I'll be whatever you say. Brother, father, uncle. How about second cousin, twice removed?" He lifted her into his arms and crossed to the steps leading upstairs. "Even if I'm a second cuz it can still be like old times. We'll sit right here and you can tell me all your problems. We can talk." A small sob shook Callie's frame and he amended, "Or cry."

His compassion was the final straw. She buried her face against his bare shoulder and wept. The grief she'd kept bottled up inside through the frantic time preceding Maudie's death and the days immediately following it came pouring out. Out and all over Julian. Not that he seemed to mind. He pulled a tattered tissue from his pocket and offered it to her.

"Thanks," Callie murmured. She scrubbed at her cheeks and blew her nose. "You're soaking wet," she thought to mention, brushing her hand across Julian's shoulders. "I didn't mean to drown you."

"No problem. Drip-dry shoulders are a prerequisite for bro—second cousins, twice removed. Although I much prefer a drenching for Maudie's sake than Tommy Lee Taylor's."

"Tommy Lee? Oh, I remember. I haven't thought about that in years," Callie said, and sighed. "I was seventeen and heartbroken all because Tommy had invited Cynthia Bentley to the prom instead of me. You found me down by the lake crying my eyes out." She bit her lip, then remembering with a guilty pang, added, "You missed your final and almost flunked your accounting course because of that."

"It was the only C I ever got and I'm damned proud of it, too." He ruffled her hair with a gentle hand. "Besides, I managed to escort the prettiest girl in all of Willow to her senior prom *and* save our trout from a salty death."

A hiccuped laugh escaped her. "A regular knight in shining armor, aren't you?"

"That's me."

She glanced at Julian from the corner of her eye. His glasses rested on top of his head, half-buried in his hair. The short crisp strands, so dark a brown they were almost black, curled stubbornly about the squared-off frames. Without his glasses his face had a sharper definition, his gaze a more piercing quality. Yet strangely, their absence also made him less the aloof businessman and more the Julian who'd captured every girlish heart at South Willow High.

"This whole business hasn't been easy for you. I'm sorry," he said with regret. "I wasn't there when you needed me and I'd give anything to change that."

"Don't apologize. You weren't to know," she hastened to reassure him. "I managed. And at least Maudie's first request is taken care of."

"Maudie's *first* request?"

Callie cleared her throat. "Oh, that's right. I haven't mentioned the requests yet, have I?"

Julian's tone was wry. "I have a funny feeling I'd remember if you'd told me."

"True enough." Callie shifted to a more comfortable position and folded her hands in her lap. "Would you like me to tell you about them now?"

He sighed in resignation. "Please."

"Before Maudie died she requested I use her notes and reminiscences for the memorial service."

"Her celebration."

Callie nodded. "That part—the celebration—was the easiest of her requests to honor."

Julian raised an eyebrow. "Easy? I doubt that. To stand up there all alone, in front of a huge crowd of people, and speak about Maudie the way you did? It must have been very difficult."

She dropped her head to his shoulder and murmured, "Not as difficult as her next request will be."

"Let me guess," he said ironically. "It has something to do with the house repairs. Am I right?"

"Yes," she admitted. "When Maudie first started on the repairs, she sat down and wrote out everything she wanted done. She left dozens of notes about it. In the hospital she asked me to finish the project." Callie shrugged. "I couldn't refuse."

"No, of course you couldn't. I'm not sure you'd know how."

She offered him an impish smile. "I know how. I just haven't had a lot of practice at it."

"At least you'll have my help on this request. It bothers me to think of your dealing with all these problems on your own." A muscle jerked in his cheek. "What happened to my father and your mother? No doubt they had their reasons for not coming to the memorial service. What was Dad's excuse this time?"

She hesitated. She'd much rather explain about Maudie's third request, but now might not be the best time. Julian didn't look in the mood to hear about juvenile delinquents and community-service hours and such. Maybe she'd tell him tomorrow. She answered his question instead. "Your father's off on a dig in some remote area of South America and can't get away."

Julian didn't bother to hide his derision. "So what else is new? He's always off on a dig in some remote part of the world. What about your mother? I don't suppose memorial services-cum-picnics are her scene. She still in L.A.? Or is it London?"

"New York."

"And she couldn't manage to come? She just left you to handle it all on your own?" There was a fierce edge to his voice, his words more a condemnation than a question.

"She sent flowers."

Callie suspected his anger was only partially aimed at their respective parents. They both knew what Helene and Jonathan were like, just as they knew their parents wouldn't change. But Julian had always had a strong sense of duty. At a guess, the greater portion of his anger was directed at himself, for what he perceived as his failure to be there when he was most needed.

She laid her hand on his arm, feeling the tension that held his muscles rigid beneath her palm. She spoke in a gentle teasing fashion. "Mother sent this huge ghastly display of lilies. And you know how much Maudie hated lilies. At least, she hated them as much as Maudie could hate anything."

He raised an eyebrow. "What did you do with Helene's poor flowers?"

Callie opened her eyes wide. "Why nothing. Much. They're doing just beautifully as mulch for the garden."

Julian laughed and relaxed back against the wooden riser of the step. "I think Maudie would have appreciated that. She always did have an offbeat sense of humor. I remember one time..." His words trailed off and he shook his head, unwilling—or unable—to finish the story. A corner of his mouth quirked upward. "Lord, I miss her."

Callie rested her head on Julian's shoulder once again, her arms sliding up and around his neck. She could hear the slow steady thump of his heart against her ear. He inhaled deeply, almost painfully it seemed, and she squeezed her eyes shut, his pain her own.

"Me too, Julian," she agreed in a quiet voice. "I can't believe she's gone." His arms tightened about her and she clung to him, sharing his grief.

She didn't know how long they sat there like that. Nor did she know when her feelings of consolation were replaced by a new sensation. It crept up on her, this change. One moment she was in the arms of her brother, and the next he'd become a man she didn't quite recognize—a man holding her to his bare chest in the sweetest of embraces.

"Julian..." The sound of her voice stirred the air between them.

She felt his lips brushing the top of her head, his cheek skimming the sensitive skin along her temple. His warm breath teased her hair and she began to tremble. She struggled against the confusion gripping her, knowing that somehow her anguish over Maudie and her need for comfort had become confused with something else. She wanted reassurance, not this strange awareness. She shivered, helpless to conceal her reaction from him.

"It's all right, Callie. I feel the same way you do," he murmured.

His mouth was close to her ear and she couldn't seem to stop shaking. "You do?" she whispered in surprise. Her eyes fluttered closed and she wished herself well away from here—someplace where she could get things back to the way they were.

Julian sighed. "It will pass, I promise. Just give it time." He slid his hand to the nape of her neck, the gentle stroke of his fingers hypnotic.

A feeling of relief surged through her. What she felt was normal. Of course. How silly of her not to realize that. "How do you know?" she demanded. "How can you be so sure it'll go away?"

"Because I felt the same way about my mother. It took time, but the feelings did pass."

Callie's eyes flew open. "What?"

"When my mother died I felt the same way you do over Maudie." He squeezed her shoulder reassuringly. "But once you work through the grieving process you tend to remember the good times, rather than the sad. It really is true that time heals all wounds."

"Oh, no," Callie choked. She tried to scramble off his lap, desperate to put some space between them. She really had gone insane. If Julian ever suspected what she'd thought . . . how she'd felt . . .

He'd laugh himself silly, that's what he'd do. Which is exactly what she'd do—as soon as she got away from him, cried herself to sleep and slept for forty-eight hours. She'd laugh about it. Sure she would.

Julian caught her hands in his, refusing to let her go. "Listen. You may not consider me your brother anymore, but I still have perfect crying shoulders. You're welcome to use them anytime. Okay?''

She nodded, her face ablaze. He tugged at her hands, urging her closer, and planted a tender kiss on her forehead. Then he rose to his feet and reached out to tuck a strand of hair behind her ear.

"Try and get some sleep, Callie. Everything will look better in the morning." With that, he turned and climbed the stairs to his room.

Of course it'll look better in the morning, she thought miserably. *How could it possibly look any worse?*

A DAMP DOGGY KISS woke Callie the next morning. "Not yet, Brutus. I'm still tired," she said in a sleepy voice. Rolling over, she shut her eyes again.

Brutus dropped his head onto her bed and sighed. He lifted his huge paw and rested it alongside her hip, nudging her until she responded.

"Cut it out," Callie protested, not wanting to wake up but not quite sure why she felt that way. She was tired, true, but that didn't explain her reluctance to— She shot straight up in bed, her memory returning in a flash of uncomfortable images.

"Julian," she said aloud. She and Julian... and the cemetery... and the steps. Callie drew her knees up to her chest and groaned, burying her head in her arms.

Brutus scrambled onto the covers and shoved his nose into the circle of her arms, forcing her to look up.

"What? You want to know what happened after you deserted me last night?" she asked the anxious dog. "I made a total fool of myself, that's what happened." She struggled out from under the massive body trying to take up permanent residence on top of her. "There I sat, on Julian's lap no less, feeling all prickly and strange, when he—"

Brutus growled low in his chest.

"Not that, you silly thing." Callie gave him a fierce hug, brandy cask and all, burying her face in the thick tan-and-white coat covering his shoulders. "Julian's been a perfect gentleman. He tried to comfort me. I'm the one who's gone off the deep end, reacting the way I did. I must be going crazy."

Brutus snorted, apparently agreeing with her.

"Give me a break, will you?" she said in offended tones. "It's because of Maudie that I'm so mixed up. My circuitry's gone haywire. I ... I'm in emotional overload. Once things calm down, so will my feelings for Julian. It's only natural I'd turn to my only brother in my time of need."

She shoved Brutus away and glared at him. "That's a disgusting noise! And yes, I said 'brother.' It was a big mistake thinking he wasn't. Look what's happened because of it—as if I didn't have enough to worry about. Now get off the bed and turn around."

She waited until Brutus had done as she requested before hopping up and stripping off her nightgown. She dressed quickly, sparing a few minutes to brush out her hair and tie it back with a bright red ribbon—for Maudie.

Callie nibbled on her lip, wishing the night before had never happened. How could she face Julian? It was too humiliating. He'd probably known all along how she felt and only pretended otherwise to save her from embarrassment. He wouldn't have to worry about it any longer, she resolved.

"Starting today, Julian's nothing more than a brother to me," she announced to Brutus. "That's it. No more funny sensations. No more goose bumps or butterflies. When I look at him it'll be like looking at ... at chocolate cake. It may be yummy but I don't have to eat it."

Brutus rolled his eyes and moaned, his long pink tongue lolling out the side of his mouth.

Callie hesitated. When *was* the last time she'd managed to pass up a slice of chocolate cake? Valerie's birthday party? No. She'd had two pieces that night. The end-of-school celebration? She shook her head, realizing that she couldn't remember the last time she'd been able to resist it. Perhaps that wasn't the best analogy to use, after all.

She eyed Brutus sternly. "You know what I'm trying to say. So I don't want to hear another word on the subject. He has his book to write and we have Maudie's notes to take care of."

She crossed to her nightstand and pulled out the small square drawer, upending it on the bed. Dozens of slips of paper cascaded over the sheets. "Okay. Let's see what we've got here. Which one shall we work on today?"

Brutus joined her by the bed and waited while she arranged the bits of paper face up and spread them out in neat rows. He examined each in turn, then picked one up in his mouth and dropped it in Callie's lap.

"The dining room?" she asked. "Are you sure? It's a lot of work. Maybe we should finish up in the study, first. Julian didn't seem very happy about the lack of walls in there."

Stubbornly Brutus shook his head, and Callie yielded with a little sigh. "Maudie did seem anxious we get that room done. Okay. We'll do it your way, but you'll have to explain it to Julian when he finds out."

A door slammed downstairs and Brutus trotted away from her, his ears cocked. He looked over his shoulder and gave a little bark before charging out of the room. Callie jumped up and hurried after him.

The first thing she saw as she headed down the stairs was Julian. The bare-chested rumpled-haired "brother" of the night before no longer existed. In his place stood an elegant sophisticated stranger. He wore another suit, this one a deep brown. The dark gold tie he'd knotted at the neck of his shirt reflected the faint pinstripe in the suit. He'd stationed himself at the foot of the steps with his arms folded across his chest. He raised one eyebrow inquiringly, staring at something out of her range of view.

With confused dismay Callie realized the sensations she'd felt for him, far from dissipating overnight, were back full force. All she could think as she watched him was that she had a sudden overwhelming craving for chocolate cake. Her stomach began to grumble.

At just that moment, he turned and saw her. "There you are. Good. Your little, ah, work detail wandered in a few minutes ago. I was just about to go up and get you."

She continued down the stairs and joined him, noticing the two sixteen-year-old high-school students who made up Maudie's third request. She could understand the doubtful tone in Julian's voice. The two didn't exactly inspire confidence.

Donna, her blond hair streaked with shocking shades of pink and purple, stood gazing at Julian as though he were a watering hole and she'd been lost in the desert for three weeks. Cory, Donna's biker boyfriend, looked on and glowered, slapping his motorcycle gloves against his jeans.

Oh, dear. This little scenario did not bode well for their day. Perhaps she shouldn't explain the particulars surrounding Cory and Donna's presence at Willow's End. Why borrow trouble? She glanced at Julian and his narrow-eyed expression. She definitely wouldn't bother him about it. Not today. Julian had enough on his plate without worrying about this. What a relief she hadn't mentioned it to him last night.

"You're leaving?" she asked with a guileless smile.

Julian nodded. "Yes. But I want to talk to you before I go." He gave one final skeptical look at her "detail" and led the way into the study. "About your workers—"

"It sure is hard to find good help these days," Callie said brightly.

"So I noticed. Which is why I don't think having those kids—"

"Fortunately for me, they're affordable." She gave an embarrassed shrug, worried he would put his foot down over Donna and Cory and she'd be forced to explain that final request. "In fact, they're all I can afford." She didn't lie. Free help, even if that constituted court-appointed free help, came well within the definition of affordable.

Julian hesitated an instant, then nodded reluctantly. "If it means getting this place in shape, I guess they'll have to do." He took a quick look around the study and for the first time Callie began to see the room through his eyes. It wasn't a pretty picture.

The plaster had been completely stripped from the walls, and shattered chunks of it lay scattered on the floor. To Callie's relief Julian didn't look too closely at the exposed beams—missing the dry rot uncovered by a few strategic pokes of a screwdriver. Instead he gazed up at the chandelier, which hung drunkenly from frayed wires.

Julian glanced from the ceiling to her and then to the water-damaged floorboards, warped into wavelike ridges. "This is interesting," he said. "New, isn't it?"

"We had a small leak."

"Uh-huh. And Noah got caught in a spring shower." With some deliberation he turned his back on the worst of the mess and addressed the issue at hand. "Maudie's lawyer agreed to see me this morning. I'm hoping, despite what you told me, that he'll have a copy of her will—or know where she might have kept it. I also want to make sure we've covered all the loose ends."

"That sounds reasonable," Callie agreed with caution.

"Thanks," came his dry response. "In the meantime, I'd appreciate it if you'd keep an eye open for her will while you and your helpers clean up around here. I can't stress how vital it is that we find it.''

"No problem. It'll turn up."

He looked as if he wanted to dispute that. Instead he shook his head, saying, "I know I told you I'd help with Maudie's second request, but these repairs are more extensive than I realized. Are you sure you can handle them along with all your other projects?"

"Of course I can!"

He eyed her doubtfully. "I don't know, Callie. I think you should hold off doing anything further until we've had time to analyze the situation. This sort of endeavor takes a lot of time, not to mention money. Have you factored that in?"

Callie bit down on her lower lip, wishing he hadn't brought up that small bothersome issue—money. Finances had become rather tight recently. Not that he needed to sound so pessimistic. "Julian—"

"I'll tell you what. Let's play it by ear and see how it goes. Fair enough?"

"Fine," she agreed, relieved.

"We'll need to get busy if we're going to find that will, fix this place up and still leave me enough time to finish my book on deadline. I'd also like to discuss the plans you and Maudie drew up for organizing these repairs."

"Plans?"

"You know. Your system." He frowned. "You *do* have a system?"

"Right. My system." She offered him a brilliant smile. That settled that. Telling him about the third request was a definite no go. Given any luck Cory and Donna would serve out their sentence with Julian none the wiser. And she could remain none the wiser about his reaction had she told him. "Why don't we discuss systems and plans and all that stuff later?" she suggested.

Julian checked his watch and nodded. "You're right. I don't have the time right now. It should keep until this afternoon."

"This afternoon," she repeated, relieved that she had a few hours to come up with something that could pass for Julian's idea of a system.

Apparently sensing her concern, he threw an arm around her shoulders and gave her a quick hug. "Don't worry. We'll work it out. But I should really get a move on."

Together, they headed for the hallway, where Julian gazed doubtfully at the waiting teens. "Good luck getting this place cleaned up. I'll be interested to see what you're able to do." With that he leaned down and gave Callie a kiss on the forehead and left.

Callie pretended not to hear Donna's blissful little sigh. Her wide-eyed glazed expression was a bit more difficult to ignore. Fortunately it seemed that Cory didn't care for Donna's reaction, either.

"Snap out of it, blondie." He poked Donna in the ribs, his black brows drawn together. "You bat those baby blues of yours any faster and your eyelashes will be airborne. What do you see in that old geezer, anyway?"

"He's not an old geezer!" Donna cried indignantly. She turned to Callie for confirmation. "He's not much older than you, is he? I mean he's more...you know, but he's not *old*."

"He has six years on me," Callie admitted with an unwarranted amount of satisfaction. "He turned thirty last month."

"Thirty?" Donna looked crestfallen for a brief moment, then brightened. "He doesn't look thirty. Maybe he's one of those types who never seem to age."

Cory snorted. "Yeah, for sure. I took one look at the guy and said to myself, now there's a man who never seems to age. He looks thirty now and I'll bet five years from now, Callie's brother won't look a day over thirty-five. Get real.''

Ex-brother, Callie almost said aloud, then remembered she'd changed her mind about that. Julian was still her brother. She sighed. This was beginning to get confusing.

"Come on," she said before Donna could catch her breath to argue. "Let's get going on today's project."

Cory slung his black leather jacket over his shoulder. "I don't suppose you made some more of those chocolate-chip cookies?" he asked with boyish greed. "They sure were good."

Callie smiled at his hopeful expression. "In the kitchen."

"Do you think we could try out a new home perm?" Donna piped up, fluffing her neon-tinted locks. "Mom doesn't always have time—what with her work schedule and all."

"We'll make time," Callie assured her. "Shall we start work?"

At their ready assent she led the way into the dining room, feeling a tiny twinge of guilt that she wasn't following Julian's instructions. He *had* been rather insistent that everything be put back together again as soon as possible. And she'd do it, too—as soon as *she* decided it was possible.

"Brutus selected the dining room for today's project," Callie informed them. "Of course, that means tearing down more walls."

"Great!" Cory exclaimed, rubbing his hands together. "Mass destruction. My favorite part."

She frowned at him. "Don't get too enthusiastic about it. That's what got you on this work detail in the first place. The little number you did with the spray cans down by the dock was the final straw as far as the judge was concerned."

"Oh, yeah, right," Cory muttered.

Callie eyed each one in turn, speaking with a sternness contrary to her nature. "Just remember the only reason you two aren't in juvey hall is because Maudie agreed to accept responsibility for your future behavior. It's either working here or spending the summer in Willow's resort for wayward teens. If you're lucky, the judge will allow me to stand in for Maudie. But I have to agree to it first. So keep me agreeable."

Cory shot her a cocky grin. "If tearing down walls keeps you agreeable, I'm all for it!"

SEVERAL HOURS LATER, Donna poked her permed pink-and-purple head into the kitchen, watching as Callie poured lemonade into three tall glasses. "Hey, Callie. We're through in the dining room. You want to see?"

"Sure do. Here, take a glass."

"Thanks." Donna picked one up and took a quick sip. "We were real careful this time. We even cleaned up everything when we finished." She opened the door to the dining room with something of a flourish.

Callie glanced around, impressed. "This looks great," she said, handing Cory his glass of lemonade.

The two had done a fantastic job. First, they'd stripped off the ugly black paneling covering the walls. Next, they'd pulled the lath-and-plaster wallboard off the two-by-four support studs. Finally, they'd cleaned away the chunks of plaster and scraps of lumber, filling a dozen industrial-strength plastic bags. They'd even opened the windows to vent the dust lingering in the air.

Cory grinned at her satisfied expression. "Everything's done except taking the trash to the dump. We decided to leave that for you. You can't expect us to do it *all*."

Callie laughed. "Heaven forbid."

"Do you think your brother will like what we did?" Donna asked eagerly. Cory rolled his eyes and groaned, impervious to Donna's glare of annoyance.

Callie struggled to hide her amusement. As reluctant as she was to shatter the illusions of her young lovestruck helper, Callie had a sneaking suspicion she'd have trouble just *explaining* the condition of the dining room to Julian, much less getting him to *like* it.

"Julian's going to love it," Callie informed Donna, attempting to sound confident. She scanned the room one final time.

It never ceased to amaze her, the difference walls made to the overall appearance. Without them, the remaining two-by-four studs were all that framed the room—that and the ancient tube-and-knob electrical wiring running between the wooden beams. Faulty electrical wiring, too. At some point the entire house would need a complete upgrade. But for now...

She glanced at Cory. "Will your brother be able to come by tomorrow and start rewiring in here and in the study?"

"He can't wait." Cory picked up the hammers and crowbars scattered around the room and put them in the toolbox. "He says it'll be great experience for when he's a real electrician."

"Good." Callie nodded. "Tell him bright and early tomorrow."

"No problem. Ten o'clock it is. What will we work on while Ted does the electrical?" He grinned mischievously, a black brow raised in question. "Or hasn't Brutus decided yet?"

Callie refused to be baited. She'd grown accustomed to being teased about Brutus, but it hadn't changed her mind about his talents one iota. "I'll let you know tomorrow," she informed him blandly. "Who knows? Maybe we'll pull apart the floors instead of the walls!"

And maybe Julian would pull her apart.

She removed Maudie's latest note from her pocket—one they'd found hidden in the dining room—and studied it. The repairs wouldn't be a problem. Not once he read the note and realized it was the logical way to find the will. Julian appreciated logic. Julian understood logic.

Julian lived, breathed and ate logic.

CHAPTER FOUR

Rule #6:
*Learn to cut your losses,
or prepare to find yourself
on the short end of the stick.*

LATER THAT AFTERNOON, Callie peeked into the oven to check on her baking for the school fund-raiser. "Yes, Mayor Fishbecker," she said, balancing the phone as she closed the oven door on the not-quite-done cakes. "I do think the statue of your grandfather is looking a bit dingy. I quite agree. Something should be done about it."

Valerie came up beside her. "Callie," she whispered urgently. "You promised to help *me*. Tell the mayor to get a scrub brush and a bucket of hot soapy water and stop wasting your time."

"A hundred-dollar donation?" Callie hesitated, remembering the dwindling balance in her checking account. "Gee, Mayor, that seems awfully steep—"

"Jingle's Hardware has buckets, soap and scrub brushes, all for under five bucks. Tell him that."

"Well, I guess I could manage fifty."

"*Fifty?* What does he want to do, gold plate it?"

"Raise the money for you? You mean, call people and ask for a donation? Maybe I— You're welcome, but— Mayor? Hello?" Callie hung up the phone and stared at it. "Well, I suppose it wouldn't hurt to make a few phone calls."

Valerie shook her head. "No one in their right mind is going to donate a plugged nickel to clean that old statue of the mayor's."

"I did," Callie said absently, sitting down at the kitchen table and adding the mayor's request to an already lengthy list.

"That's because everyone knows you're an easy touch." Valerie gave an exasperated sigh. "Could we finish our conversation before anyone else calls? Can you baby-sit Danny tomorrow or not?"

"Sure. Let me add it to my list."

"No! Don't do that, it'll get lost. I'll tack a reminder to the refrigerator door," Valerie said, putting words into action. "I've got to run." She paused and eyed Callie sternly, her hands on her hips. "You won't forget now, will you?"

"I won't. I promise."

"Just checking." Valerie flashed Callie an impish grin. "I wouldn't want you to forget Danny the way you have those cakes." She sniffed the air. "I do believe something's burning." And with that, she made a hasty exit.

CALLIE HEARD A CAR pull into the driveway just as a clock somewhere in the depths of the house struck four. She scraped the final smidgen of icing from the mixing bowl and spread it over the top of the cake.

"Julian's home," she informed Brutus, although he clearly didn't need any warning.

The Saint Bernard peeked out from his hiding place in the pantry and attempted a growl, though the noise that escaped him sounded more like a whimper. With an embarrassed snort he backed out of sight.

"You're being ridiculous, you know." She licked the last of the chocolate icing off the spatula. "If Maudie saw you slinking around like that she'd be downright ashamed. I told you, Julian was just kidding about the baseball bat. Can't you take a joke?''

A sharp bark erupted from the pantry.

''Well, you better not desert me today the way you did last night,'' she warned him, carrying her baking paraphernalia to the sink. ''I told you what happened because of it. And now look what I've gone and done.''

She glanced at the four cakes and wiped the perspiration from her brow. With the heat steadily building throughout the day, she'd been crazy to bake four when Suzanne Ashmore only needed three for the school fund-raiser—especially after she'd burned the first two.

That extra cake would be a problem. No. The real problem would be limiting herself to a single slice. Her craving for chocolate had reached insatiable levels—something she couldn't remember ever happening before.

The front door slammed and Callie tilted her head to one side, listening to the distinctive rhythm of Julian's footsteps. They resounded first in the hallway, and then on the stairs as he climbed to the second floor. Good. Maybe she'd have time for a piece of cake before he came looking for her. That way she could fortify herself against any further...cravings.

Julian returned downstairs just as she put a second forkful of the gooey confection in her mouth. She snatched up her glass of milk, hurriedly washing the cake down. Time to switch to her ''sister'' mode—and time to discover how much Julian appreciated the fine job done on the dining room.

Brutus poked his nose out of the pantry and they both waited for Julian's reaction.

He walked down the hallway, passing the dining room without pausing and continued on his way to the kitchen.

Callie grinned at Brutus. ''See? And you were worried about what he might say. Julian understands all about redecorating. In fact, I wouldn't be surprised if he's really impressed with what we've done. Trust me."

She relaxed back in her chair for a whole two seconds—until she heard his footsteps stop with nerve-racking abruptness, then retrace themselves. She listened, straining to hear an indication—any indication—of his reaction to their efforts.

A loud thin wail pierced the awful silence as he pushed open the dining-room door. *That isn't Julian,* Callie reassured herself. *It's only a squeaky hinge.* She swallowed, her throat inexplicably dry.

The noisy echo of shoes striking the wood flooring in the vacant room was unmistakable. *Okay, he's gone in,* she determined, *and he's looking around.* He'd make a slow leisurely examination of the wonderful job they'd done. Next he'd notice how carefully they'd swept up the debris, how thoroughly they'd pulled all the nails out of the wooden two-by-fours, how much—

"Cal-lie!"

Brutus gave a hoarse yip and barreled out of the pantry, knocking over a shelf of canned goods, a stack of paper towels, a bucket and a mop. He broke into the kitchen at a gallop, upending two chairs in his path. As graceful as a gazelle with a wooden leg, he leapt over a third chair and landed square on top of a throw rug. Aladdin on his flying carpet couldn't have done better; Brutus sailed majestically across the kitchen floor, past Callie, and out the back screen door, a can of chili rolling in his wake.

"You can't do this to me again!" Callie cried. She jumped to her feet and raced to the back door. It was too late. Brutus was nowhere to be seen. "You...you...back stabber!"

"Exactly." Julian stalked into the kitchen. Two dark red patches of color rode high on his cheeks. His eyes flashed with black wrath. "*What* have you done to the dining room? No. Strike that. I know what you've done to the dining room. What I want to know is why. *Why* did you rip it all apart? No. Strike that. I can even guess why you did your best to gut the place, despite my explicit instructions. It's because of Maudie's request, isn't it?"

Callie opened her mouth to reply, then shut it as he continued his diatribe.

"Damn it, Callie! Have you any idea the time and money it's going to take to get this house back into shape? You can't have. Because if you did, you wouldn't have ripped apart another room." His gaze fell on the table and he snatched up her list, examining it carefully. "I can't believe this. On top of everything else, you're supposed to do all these things?" He glared at her in disbelief. "I think I understand—finally. You don't know what you're doing. Anything anyone wants from you, you give them. That's it, isn't it?"

He was furious, yet even in a rage, Callie found him irresistible. His jeans were old and tight, hugging his narrow hips and muscled thighs like a lover. His short-sleeved cotton shirt emphasized the breadth of his shoulders and the power of his biceps.

Callie sighed. Julian's chameleonlike changes from sophistication to casual informality were beginning to play havoc with her emotions. She wished he'd stick to one image. She glanced longingly at the kitchen table—and the four cakes. Four was *not* going to be enough.

"Callie, have you listened to a single word I've said?"

"No," she admitted. "Those cakes are calling to me. Would you like a piece?"

He stared at her in silence, then shook his head, clearly at a loss. Without another word he returned her list to the table, righted the two chairs Brutus had knocked over and picked up the can of chili, setting it on the counter. He strode to the back door and went out.

Callie's brows drew together in concern. She'd hurt his feelings, she realized with growing dismay. At the very least she'd insulted him. But he didn't understand. If only she didn't find him so...distracting. She'd thought that baking the cakes would help, but it only made her think about him all the more.

It was her emotional circuitry going haywire again, she decided with a grimace. Maybe when Cory's brother came tomorrow he could rewire her, as well as the dining room. She hurried to the back door.

She could see Julian walking down by the lake, his hands shoved deep in his pockets, his head bent in thought. Brutus, curiosity causing his ears to twitch every so often, trailed after Julian, keeping a cautious distance between them.

Callie sighed. It was all her fault. He wouldn't be feeling so out of sorts if it weren't for her. She should go out and explain about Maudie and her latest note....

Pushing open the screen door, she stepped outside. The intensity of the heat took her by surprise. The humidity must be close to a hundred percent, she thought, perspiration coating her skin with tiny beads of moisture. She crossed the broad green expanse of grass to the edge of the lake. Once there, she kicked off her shoes and bent to roll up the cuffs of her jeans.

"Julian, wait," she called down the beach, splashing through the shallows to his side. He, too, was barefoot, and kept walking, but Callie didn't let that deter her. "Julian, I'm sorry. I didn't mean to make you angry."

"I'm not angry," he denied, walking steadily toward a stand of willow trees that bordered the lake.

"How about, disappointed, irritated, frustrated..." She saw him pause and realized she'd hit the appropriate word.

"Frustrated. I'm sorry I frustrate you. I don't mean to." She searched his face, trying to read his expression. A few years ago that would have been a simple task. Now, it was next to impossible.

"We need to talk," he said abruptly. "This nonsense can't continue. We are going to sit down, right this minute, and make some decisions about that house." He looked at her, his gaze direct and determined. "Because the way things stand right now, I don't see how you can possibly keep Willow's End—no matter who inherits."

"No!" Callie cried, staring at Julian in alarm, the full import of his words sinking in. "You can't mean... You're not suggesting we *sell* Willow's End? You can't be serious!"

"I'm very serious. Sit down."

The heat shimmered in a hazy curtain, making her acutely aware of the intense humidity. An inconsistent breeze did nothing to alleviate the oppressiveness. Her gaze sought out Brutus. She was reassured to find him close at hand. He stood in a field of clover, snapping at the noisy bumblebees that labored diligently over each white flower.

Without a word, she dropped to a shady spot beneath the trees and waited for him to speak, praying she'd misunderstood him. Nervously, she picked up a whiplike willow twig and began to methodically strip off the neat symmetrical row of light green leaves.

Julian sat down beside her. "I understand your desire to honor Maudie's wishes," he began, choosing his words with care. "And I know how much Willow's End means to you. But we need to be practical." As though realizing how much his words must hurt her, he reached out and gave her shoulder a squeeze.

For him, the innocent touch was an act of comfort, or perhaps sympathy. Callie knew he hadn't a clue about the storm of reactions it set off within her. She stared down at her hands gripping the willow twig, afraid to so much as move.

Why wasn't the chocolate cake working? She glanced at Julian. He was a lot of man. Perhaps it took a lot of cake to compensate for that.

When she didn't reply, he continued, "I assumed that you and Maudie had an organized system for these repairs." He fixed her with an ironic look. "Foolish of me, I admit."

"That's not true," Callie claimed, finding her voice at last. *Focus on Maudie and the repairs,* she told herself. *The sooner this conversation is over, the sooner you can get back to the kitchen—and the cake.* "I told you Maudie left notes telling me what to do."

Julian shook his head. "Yet you seem to leap from one project to the next, as though you're pulling her instructions out of a hat."

He saw Callie's start of surprise and gave an incredulous laugh. "You're joking! Tell me you don't do it that way."

"If you must know, it's a drawer, not a hat," she muttered, prudently avoiding any mention of Brutus. Instead she attempted to explain. "I didn't think it mattered which room we pulled apart first, since they all have to be done." Judging by Julian's reaction, she'd have been better off mentioning Brutus, Callie realized.

"They *all* have to be done? Why?"

She cleared her throat and tossed her stripped willow twig into the grass. "Because of the faulty electrical wiring." She watched nervously as Julian struggled to control his anger.

"Faulty electrical wiring?" he ground out. "As well as a leaky roof, new walls, exterior and interior painting jobs, dry rot—yes, I saw the dry rot in the study—and Lord know's what else?" He shot her a furious glance. "Callie, how much money do you have in your account?"

"I...I'm not exactly sure."

"How much?"

Callie jumped, speaking in a rush. "About fifty-six dollars and eight cents." She paused, remembering the mayor. "Less the fifty-dollar donation to help clean Mayor Fishbecker's statue. I guess that leaves—"

"Six dollars and eight cents." His anger drained away, compassion taking its place. "Have you any idea what it will cost to get Willow's End back into shape?" When she shook her head he mentioned a figure that staggered her.

"But Maudie said she could handle the improvements," Callie protested.

"She probably could have," he agreed. "She had a small annuity that might just have covered the repairs, provided she spaced them out over time. But until we find the will, we won't know whether she took the possibility of her death into consideration when planning them. Bottom line: whoever inherits the house also inherits the expense of the repairs. Somehow, I don't think that's an expense you're capable of carrying."

Callie bit her lip. "No," she admitted in a quiet voice. "It's not." Then she gazed hopefully at him. "You're not sure, though, about the money. There might be enough."

"Or there might not. In this case I'd rather err on the side of caution." He tucked a strand of chestnut-brown hair behind her ear and spoke gently. "Sweetheart, don't you realize it's too much for you? It's not just the money—or possible lack of it. You can't cope with any of the things you've taken on, or with the people who take advantage of your generosity."

She firmed her lips into a stubborn line. "I can manage."

He raised an eyebrow. "Can you? You have fifty dollars to your name and you give it away. You have a list of tasks sitting on the kitchen table that would stagger an army. The repairs to the house are monumental and totally unorganized. Don't you see that you're out of options here?

Something's got to give before you wear yourself out. There isn't any other reasonable choice but to sell."

Callie shook her head. "No, Julian. I can't. I love that house."

"I do, too," he said, "but it's only a house. What's the old saying? Home is where the heart is. You know it's the people that make the home, not the wood and brick and mortar."

Tears filled her eyes and she shook her head again. "But Willow's End isn't just a house, Julian," she whispered, her voice breaking. "It's our *home*. Please, please, don't take that away."

He reached over and put his arms around her, holding her tight against him. "I'm not taking it away. But, think about it. I'll be back in Chicago soon. You can't manage on your own. I'd worry about you."

"I'll get it all taken care of before you leave." She pulled back and looked at him. "Give me a chance to prove it to you. I *can* cope. You'll see."

He inhaled deeply, then inclined his head. "All right, Callie. We'll give it a try." He eyed her sternly. "Don't look so relieved. I still think selling is our only option. In the meantime, we need to agree on a few things."

She nodded eagerly. Deep down she knew Julian couldn't sell his home any more than she could. Once his heart overruled that logical brain of his, he'd discover that for himself. But if it would help placate him, she'd agree to shave the earth with a butter knife. "Name your conditions."

He counted off on his fingers. "First. We sit down and organize a proper plan for the repairs."

"Agreed."

"Second. You give top priority to finding that will. Third. No more donations of time or money until you take care of your current commitments."

"I can do that," she said confidently. That would be a snap. "So what's fourth and final?"

"Fourth and final." His voice took on a steely quality. "You don't remove one nail, one piece of plaster or one floorboard without my approval."

"Done." She beamed at him, relieved beyond measure. "Thank you, Julian. I don't know what I'd do if I lost Willow's End. You don't know how much it means to me."

He smiled at her and cupped her face in his hands. "I have an idea. It's a special place, isn't it? Though not nearly as special as its chief resident."

He'd taken his glasses off—when, Callie wasn't quite sure—and his eyes as they met hers were a warm dark brown. Like chocolate, she thought hazily. Thick rich chocolate.

His head lowered, and Callie knew—*knew*—he was going to offer her another of his brotherly kisses. She began to tremble, certain that this time she'd give herself away. She was too emotional, her barriers too far down to successfully hide her reaction to him. If he kissed her, she'd respond in a way he couldn't mistake—as a woman does to a man. And that would ruin everything. She jerked free of his light hold and jumped to her feet, backing toward the lake.

"Callie?" Julian stood up, frowning. "What's wrong?" He followed her, closing the gap between them.

He's going to know. He'll figure it out.

A curious glint entered his eyes and a discerning sort of smile touched the corners of his mouth. Sudden awareness, clear and unmasked, showed in his expression as he stepped determinedly after her, his intentions unmistakable. Like a predatory animal picking up a scent, he came for her. "Callie—"

"Boy, is it ever hot!" she gasped, seizing on the first thought to pop into her head. "We should go for a swim.

That would be perfect, don't you think? A nice cool swim?''

The words were no sooner out of her mouth than Brutus came charging across the meadow. He gave a single excited bark before two hundred pounds of anxious-to-please dog hit her square in the chest. Callie shrieked, her arms flailing like windmills. With a smothered oath, Julian grabbed at her, but it was too late. She fell over backward into the lake. Julian, still holding her arm, fell right along with her.

Brutus sat down on the sandy beach and grinned.

Callie surfaced, sputtering and coughing. It took three attempts, and Julian's help, to sit up. She glared at Brutus. "What did you do that for?" she croaked, searching wildly for the most horrible thing she could think of to say to him. "You . . . you stupid *dog!*"

"Oh, that's telling him," Julian snarled. "That should cut him right to the quick."

But watching Brutus, she thought perhaps it did. He howled in anguish, then raced back and forth along the shore, barking furiously. Callie chewed her lip, a sudden thought occurring to her. By pushing her into the lake at that key moment, Brutus *had* helped her. He'd provided the perfect distraction and prevented Julian from questioning her any further about her panicky reaction to his touch.

She peeked over at Julian. This was not a happy man. Not even a little bit. At a guess, Brutus's life hung by a very thin thread. She cleared her throat. "Uh, your glasses?" she probed delicately.

"Under the tree somewhere."

"I don't suppose your wallet . . ."

"On the dresser in my bedroom."

So far so good. Now for the most crucial question. "Your watch—is it waterproof by any chance?"

"So they claim." He examined the expensive timepiece and shook his wrist. "We'll know soon enough, won't we?"

Callie beamed in relief. "Then there's no problem."

"No problem?" Julian echoed. His dark brows almost met over the bridge of his nose. "No problem!" His fist hit the surface of the water, sending a spray toward shore. "Are you insane? That dog pushed us in the lake. Deliberately!" He stopped, as though aware of what he'd once again admitted. "And take that look off your face, Callie Marcus."

"What look?" she asked innocently.

"You know full well what look I'm talking about." His eyes narrowed. "I've revised my opinion of that animal," he announced. "Slightly. I'll admit—and admit only—that he's capable of premeditated deliberate acts of mayhem. And when I catch the stupid mutt, he'll find himself incapable of that, because I'm going to turn his hide into a bath mat!"

Brutus didn't wait to hear any more. With a high-pitched yowl, he took off, sand flying in his wake.

"You've frightened him," Callie reproached.

"Tough." Julian heaved himself upward, water cascading off his clothing.

"I don't understand why you're so angry. The water feels great, nice and refreshing." She shook her wet hair back from her face. "Why don't we go for a swim?"

Julian stared down at her, his hands anchored on his hips. If Callie thought his jeans clung before, it was nothing to what they did now.

She closed her eyes and tilted her face up to the burning rays of the sun. Better not to look she thought; safer. But she couldn't resist taking one more peek. She squeezed her eyes closed again. Yep, much safer not to look.

"You're crazy," he informed her. "I mean, I suspected you were moderately insane before. But that particular suggestion has proven to me beyond a shadow of a doubt that you're flat-out, round the bend crazy."

Callie lifted her chin. "I'm not crazy and neither is my idea. Not when you consider how hot it is and the fact that we're already wet. I was just about to suggest a swim when Brutus..." Best to skip that part, she decided judiciously. "So we don't have our suits on. Let's be daring and swim in our clothes."

"Forget it, Callie."

She lowered her lashes, hiding the sly gleam she knew must be there in her eyes. Only one thing could change his mind. "Bet you a slice of chocolate cake I can beat you to the raft."

She threw down the challenge like a gauntlet. It would be next to impossible for Julian to resist; at least, he'd never been able to resist a wager in the eleven years she'd known him. It was one of the first things she'd learned about him when she'd moved to Willow's End. It was also the only silly irrational thing she'd ever known Julian to do.

For a minute she didn't think he'd go for it. Then amusement replaced his irritation and he dove back into the deeper water, striking out for the raft anchored fifty feet offshore.

Callie set off after him, the heavy drag of her clothing a major handicap. Not that his clothing seemed to bother Julian. He cut cleanly through the water, outstripping her with ease. By the time she reached the raft, breathless and exhausted, she felt as if she'd run five miles.

Julian stood on the rocking wooden surface, chuckling at her futile efforts to lever herself up beside him. Then he seemed to take pity on her, for he leaned down and grabbed her hand, helping her onto the raft.

"Was that supposed to be a real bet?" he teased.

It was a full minute before she could breathe normally again. "I noticed you took me up on it," she retorted at last. "You never could resist."

He shot her an amused look and shook his head. "You mean, *you* never could resist. At thirteen you were so shy and skittish, I found our little bets were the only way I could get through to you."

She stared at him. "You mean, you don't really like to bet? You did that just for me?"

Julian sat down and stretched his long legs out in front of him. "Wagering is illogical, impractical and a total waste of time." He tossed her a grin. "Except with gorgeous brunettes who never win and make the best chocolate cake in the state. Then it's irresistible."

All these years she'd thought... And Julian had been doing it to make her feel at home. She could feel the color creeping into her face and she offered him a tremulous smile. "You're a nice man, Julian Lord."

Aware she was fast entering dangerous territory, she quickly changed the subject. "You do realize that with our clothes on we'll never make it back to shore without drowning. We'll have to spend the rest of our lives out here, eating raw fish and surviving on lake water."

"Raw fish?" Julian shook his head. "No way. I'll just wait for the Burns brothers to rescue me. They should be along any night now."

"You're forgetting," Callie reminded him gloomily, sitting down beside him. "When I blew the whistle on them at the memorial service, they were grounded. We'll be stuck here for the next fifty years."

Julian leaned back on one elbow and grinned, his voice a suggestive murmur. "Well, my sweet, since it's the weight of our clothes that's keeping us tied here, we could always peel down to the buff and swim back. Of course, the pile of clothing we leave on the raft might cause a bit of gossip.

What do you think? Could we survive being the talk of Willow?''

He sat up and in one swift movement yanked his shirt over his head and off. Callie's mouth dropped open. She'd thought he was kidding, but he intended to do it! He intended to take off his clothes and swim back to shore, buck naked.

Julian chuckled. His eyes were alight with laughter and his grin deepened the lines marking either side of his mouth. Little droplets of water glittered in hair that, uncombed and wet, curled loosely back from his brow. He touched her bright red cheeks with a fingertip.

"Relax. I was joking about skinny-dipping. I'm not planning on taking advantage of you, only of the sunshine.''

Callie didn't know whether to be relieved or sorry. He lay back on the raft and she couldn't resist staring at him. No two ways about it—this was one gorgeous male animal. Stripped of his civilized trappings, his sleek grace combined with his strong muscular body in a potent combination. And it all spelled danger, pure and simple. Spellbinding, finger-burning, irresistible danger.

She lifted her wet shirt away from her body, wishing that, like Julian, she could shed it. It clung uncomfortably to her skin, and she wiggled in response, which only made matters worse. Any minute now her jeans would start steaming beneath the hot afternoon sun. She sighed.

"Take them off. I don't mind,'' Julian said without opening his eyes.

"You know I can't do that. Someone might see.'' Worse, Julian might see. Might? No might about it. He would. She shivered, the thought chilling her where moments before she'd been sweltering from the heat.

A smile curved his mouth. "No one will see. And wet as your shirt is, it's not doing much of a job protecting your modesty, anyway."

To punctuate his comment, Julian turned his head and looked at her. His gaze swept over her body almost possessively, and for an insane moment she felt he'd branded her irrevocably as his own. His smile grew broader.

Callie looked down at herself, catching her breath in dismay. He wasn't kidding. She crossed her arms in front of her chest. "Stop staring at me!"

Julian laughed, the sound rich and husky. "It almost makes me forget you're my sister."

It was hard to breathe. "I'm not your sister," she whispered.

Something glittered deep in the dark brown of his eyes. "In that case..."

He lunged toward her, catching her by surprise. With a startled gasp, she jerked away from him and scrambled backward, forgetting they were on a raft. For a crazy moment, she teetered on the edge of the wooden boards, then, just as she started to fall, Julian pulled her into his arms.

"Easy," he murmured, cradling her to his bare chest. His voice, filled with gentle amusement, rumbled against her ear. "I was kidding. What did you think I was going to do to you?"

"Kiss me," Callie answered him. She stopped breathing altogether, horrified by both her confession and her apparent demand. "I mean, I thought you were *going* to kiss me. I didn't mean for you ... for you to actually ... *do* it." She waited in dread for his laugh.

He didn't laugh. Instead he cupped her chin and raised her face to his. "And that sent you into such a panic? Why? I've kissed you before."

As though to remind her, his lips touched her temple with a feather-light caress. Callie's lids fluttered down and she sighed, desire and curiosity getting the better of her. Perhaps a kiss wasn't such a bad idea. She wanted it, craved it, in fact. A kiss from Julian might prove the perfect way of working him out of her system.

She relaxed into his embrace, her hands inching up his chest until they clung to his shoulders. His skin felt warm and smooth against her fingers, the muscles beneath, rock solid. He held her close to him, his arms tight and protective.

His jaw brushed her cheek with an abrasive rasp, and Callie gasped at the unfamiliar sensation. He moved closer, increasing her awareness of how intimately his bare chest was pressed to her thin damp shirt. As his fingers glided down the side of her neck, her breath caught in her throat.

She turned her head and looked at him. Her gaze fastened on his mouth and she stared at it, mesmerized. Unable to help herself, she raised her face until her lips were a mere hairbreadth away from his, eager to discover her reaction to his kiss. She sensed his momentary hesitation, sensed the internal debate that kept him from taking what she so readily offered. Did he still think of her as his sister?

He exhaled slowly. "Why not?" he muttered against her mouth, and kissed her.

The man could give lessons, Callie thought. And then she didn't think at all, only felt. His hand drew a leisurely path down her spine, coming to rest at her hip, molding her to him. His firm grip pulled her shirt taut against her breasts, the friction of the damp material teasing her nipples. She groaned softly at the sensation, shivering beneath his touch, helpless to do more than follow where he led.

And lead he did. He cupped her jaw, the brush of his thumb easing her lips apart. Her mouth moved eagerly beneath his, opening to his warmth, his gentleness. His need consumed her, the thoroughness of his exploration a startling experience. His skill was unquestionable—and irresistible.

But it wasn't just skill, she recognized. Something more existed between them. Till this instant she'd thought Willow's End was her true home. Now she knew differently. It felt as though a bond had been forged, a oneness. Far from getting him out of her system, she knew he'd wrought an indelible change in her. She'd never be able to think of Julian in the same way again.

With seeming reluctance he ended the kiss and pulled back. Callie couldn't conceal her regret. She opened her eyes and gazed up at him, pleased to see the remnants of passion marking his face. Color rode high on his cheeks and his dark eyes glittered with satisfaction. He'd felt it too, this link between them.

He traced the arch of her brow with a gentle finger. "I've never seen your eyes look so green. They're beautiful." He smoothed a strand of damp hair back from her face. "It's amazing the changes a few years can bring about." He cocked his head to one side. "But I think it's time to talk, don't you?"

She could only nod, too nervous to reply. They did need to talk. This new feeling they shared had changed things.

He rubbed his shadowed jaw. "Now, then. Let's get serious about Maudie and her will. We've a lot to accomplish in less than two months—which doesn't leave us much time for fun and games."

CHAPTER FIVE

Rule #12:
Emotion is like a boiling pot.
Both need lids,
and neither belongs in business.

CALLIE'S EYES WIDENED in hurt disbelief. Fun and games? Was that all their kiss had meant to him? Hadn't he felt any of the pleasure, any of the attraction, any of the special-ness of their embrace?

Apparently not. She lowered her eyes, hiding her con-fusion and dismay from his discerning gaze.

She'd read too much into his actions, Callie realized. She'd mistaken mild pleasure on his part for something more. Worse, she'd practically begged him for that kiss. Should Julian be blamed because he'd been kind enough to oblige? It all spelled a simple difference of opinion. A mis-understanding. These things happened. She caught her lip between her teeth. These things happened all the time. Didn't they?

She took a deep stabilizing breath. She didn't dare let him guess how she felt. "You're right. We should discuss Mau-die and her will," Callie agreed in a subdued voice. "Was her lawyer any help?"

Julian hesitated, as though in response to something in her words or tone. Then he shook his head. "None at all. As you surmised, Peters has no idea where Maudie stashed her will."

"Which is what I told you. So you can't be all that surprised."

"Not surprised, no," Julian admitted. "But I am disappointed. I'd hoped he'd offer some clue as to its whereabouts."

Callie gave a little shrug. "Oh, well. Not to worry." She rested her elbows on her knees, cupping her chin in one hand. "Her latest note said she hid it good and proper. So I guess we'll just have to keep searching for it."

A long moment of silence stretched between them. "You mean you found another of Maudie's notes and didn't tell me?"

Was he annoyed? Callie glanced at him. He was annoyed. "It slipped my mind," she said truthfully. "I've got it right here in my pocket." She leaned back and shoved her hand into her stiff damp jeans, pulling out a soggy matted pink piece of paper.

Julian raised his eyes skyward. "That's just great," he muttered. He stood up, his restless movements causing the raft to rock beneath them. "I don't suppose you read the note and can tell me what it said?"

"Yes, but..." She hesitated. "You won't get angry?" He gave an impatient shake of his head and Callie confessed, "She said she left a note that would reveal the location of her will. All we have to do is find the note."

"First we had to find a will, now we have to find a note?" He was clearly struggling to keep control of his temper. "What could Maudie have been thinking of?" He stared down at Callie. "Did she explain why she's done this—aside from the fact that I work too much and need a vacation? Though if this is her idea of a vacation, I think I'll stick to writing my book."

Callie avoided his gaze. "I think she might have mentioned another reason."

She cringed as he bit out, "What precisely did she mention, Callie?"

"Maudie said she was aware we'd grown apart recently and hoped this would bring us back together." She held her breath waiting for the explosion.

It never came. Instead Julian said in a calm voice, "Now that's the first reasonable thing she's said so far. Okay. Let's think this through."

He reached down and picked up his shirt, pulling it over his head. Then he ran his hands through his hair, combing the short unruly strands back into place. Callie watched the change with regret. Her Julian was fast disappearing, replaced by the superanalytical Mr. Lord. All he needed were those darned businesslike glasses to revert to the formal executive.

"Where have you found these notes?" he asked with brisk efficiency.

"Why, everywhere." At his stare of disbelief, Callie elaborated. "The notes about the will were in the study and the dining room. But her notes about the repairs she put everywhere. I've found them in drawers and under rugs, in the flour canister and under couch cushions." She shrugged. "I just gather them up when I find them and stick them with the others in my bedroom."

Julian looked at her sternly. "Considering your feelings for Willow's End, I'm amazed by your nonchalance. Perhaps this will help spark your interest. If we don't find that will, you don't inherit Willow's End. I don't inherit Willow's End. According to Peters, my father would inherit her *entire* estate, lock, stock and crazed Saint Bernard."

Impossible. Julian must be mistaken. "But—"

"Not buts about it, I'm afraid. From what I understand, if Maudie was the last one in possession of the will, and it can't be found within a reasonable period of time, the court presumes she revoked it."

He allowed that to sink in before adding, "So, my sweet, if you don't want your home sold out from under you to finance one of Jonathan's South American expeditions, you'd better help me figure out where she put that note— and the will."

Callie's eyes widened as full understanding crashed down on her. Her home. She could lose her home! She stared up at Julian in alarm. "No! We have to do something. They can't..."

If he felt any satisfaction at her change of attitude, he didn't show it. "It's all right, Callie," he said, attempting to reassure her. "We'll find it. Don't panic. All we have to do is figure out how Maudie's mind worked."

That did not sound good. Not good at all. How was she supposed to know the workings of Maudie's mind? For the first time she fully appreciated Julian's position. No wonder he'd been so upset by her attitude.

"We can handle it, Callie," he continued. "If we work together, I'm confident we can straighten out this mess."

She nodded. "Right. Work together."

He closed his eyes briefly and shook his head. "Now pay attention," he said, and his voice contained a hard edge. "This is what I want you to do. Round up those kids of yours next time they come over, and sell them on the idea of a treasure hunt. Give them the run of the place." He paused. "Within reason. But have them look for Maudie's notes."

She nodded, more than willing to cooperate. How could she have known the will would be so important? "All right, if you say so."

"I say so." Julian paced the raft, his restlessness a palpable thing. "With that book of mine to complete I only have so much time I can commit to this nonsense. I can't afford to play games—certainly not ones involving a will that might or might not exist."

A trout broke the surface of the lake, leaping for a fly, and the sun flashed off its iridescent scales. No time for games. Callie turned her head and stared out across the calm blue-green water. Kissing her had been fun and games—a waste of time. Was sitting in the sun, talking, a waste of his time, as well? Probably.

Her mouth drooped. She hated the changes in Julian over the past two years. He used to be so much fun: inventive, creative, always one with a ready laugh and a zest for life that left her breathless. He'd never before counted their pleasure in one another's company in terms of wasted minutes or hours.

When had he run out of time? He used to have all the time he needed with some to spare. But no longer. Now business was his god and time his taskmaster. Callie was just a distraction. And Julian didn't like distractions.

Callie stood up. "I should be getting dinner ready," she announced in a small voice. "I think I'll swim back now, if you don't mind."

"You're right. As enjoyable as this has been—"

"I know. It's time to get back to work," she finished for him, struggling not to show her hurt.

Julian's hand dropped to her shoulder and he pulled her around to face him. "I was going to say that as enjoyable as it's been, I don't want you to catch a chill. The trees are blocking the sun and the breeze has picked up a bit."

"Oh."

"Yes. Oh." He continued to study her expression, his hand moving gently along her arm. She couldn't suppress a shiver and, noticing it, he asked, "What's wrong, Callie? You've been acting very strangely the last hour or so."

"Nothing," she denied, wishing he wouldn't touch her. If she'd been aware of him before, it was nothing to what she felt now. His hand, warm and heavy, came to rest on the bare skin above her elbow.

"It's that kiss, isn't it?" he guessed with uncomfortable accuracy. His lips curved upward, as though savoring the memory of their embrace. Callie caught her breath at his expression, only to release it in a rush when he said, "Forget about it, okay? Pretend it never happened. I'd hate for our friendship to be ruined over such a silly incident. The misunderstanding about Gwen was bad enough, without letting something like this come between us."

A silly incident. Something like this. He'd never know how cruelly his words cut her. She lifted her chin and stepped away from him, putting on a brave smile. "You're right," she agreed. "It's foolish to let one meaningless kiss spoil things."

He grinned. "Good girl. Now take off your jeans."

She stared at him. "What?"

"You heard me. Take off your jeans."

Her heart began to pound. "Why?" She managed to get the word past a throat gone bone dry. She swallowed. "What do you want them for?"

His eyebrows shot up. "I don't want them at all. I just want you to take them off before swimming back to shore. You nearly drowned getting out here. You'll find the going much easier if you don't have twenty pounds of dead weight pulling you under."

Callie gave an emphatic shake of her head. "Forget it. I'll take my chances."

"No, you won't." Julian turned his back to her, folding his arms across his chest. "I'm not looking. I won't even peek, I promise. Strip down and leave your jeans on the raft. I'll bring them with me and you can slip them on in the shallows."

With a sigh, she unzipped the still-damp jeans and stepped clear of them, uncomfortable in only a shirt and underpants. Julian, Callie noted with mixed feelings, kept his promise and didn't move a muscle. Taking one last tantalizing look at him, she dove into the water and struck out for shore.

Even giving her a head start and hampered by the extra clothing he carried, Julian still beat her to shore. He stood on the beach watching her approach. Remembering the shortcomings of her shirt, Callie kept well down in the water.

"Could you throw me my jeans now, Julian?"

For an instant, she didn't think he would. He held them in his hand, a wicked grin on his face. Then, relenting, he tossed them to her.

"Seems a shame, though," he commented regretfully, "when I know for a fact that my, ah, cousin, twice removed, has the prettiest legs in all of Willow." With a wink, he strode off down the beach.

Callie clutched the wet jeans to her chest. "I'm not your cousin! Or your sister, either!" she shouted at his departing back. She bit down on her lip. "I guess I'm not your anything at all," she whispered.

EARLY THE NEXT MORNING, Callie slipped into the kitchen, determined to get an early start on her chores—and the list. She looked down at the floor in distaste. With all the dust stirred up by the repairs, the linoleum didn't stay clean for longer than a day or two. A thorough sweeping and swabbing was in order. Rolling up her sleeves, she set to it.

The sweeping part took no time at all, the rhythmic movement of the broom and the satisfying results giving her a feeling of accomplishment. Getting the bucket and mop from the pantry, she filled the metal container with hot soapy water and began the more prolonged chore of finding the white beneath the dingy gray of the floor. Halfway through the job, the phone rang.

"Hello, Callie?" a friendly voice greeted. "Suzanne Ashmore from the school board here. I'm calling about those cakes you promised for the fund-raiser. You were able to get them done, weren't you?''

Guilt stricken, Callie thought of the slice she'd swiped in the middle of the night. She was making definite inroads on that extra cake. Thank goodness she'd baked it, or Suzanne's fund-raiser would be short. "Sure thing. I have them all ready to go. When do you want to pick them up?''

Suzanne gave a tiny laugh. "That's the problem. I'm totally bogged down this morning and hoped you might have a spare moment to drop them off. Can I count on you to do that?''

Callie hesitated, wondering if it would violate Julian's request that she not take on any more projects. No, she decided. This was part and parcel of her fund-raiser commitment. "Sure, no problem. What time do you need them?''

"Is noon convenient?''

Callie glanced at the large expanse of floor still waiting to be cleaned and then at the long list on the kitchen table and sighed. "Noon's fine.''

"In that case," Suzanne said, "do you think you could pick up Mrs. Hankum's pies and Lu Ridgeway's corn muffins? They're right on your way.''

In for a penny, Callie thought. "Of course. No problem at all.''

The door opened behind her and she turned to see Valerie, with Danny perched on her hip. Callie waved them in. Valerie dumped the baby into Callie's arms and, after numerous incomprehensible hand signals, disappeared back out the door. A minute later she reappeared, dragging a high chair behind her.

Suzanne continued, "There's one more small matter, as long as I've got you on the line.''

"Yes? What is it?''

Valerie retrieved Danny and slipped him into the high chair, handing him some biscuits and his bottle. Planting a quick kiss on the crown of his head, she waved a cheerful farewell to Callie and left.

Danny watched his mother go, his little face puckering into a frown. The instant he realized she wasn't returning, he opened his mouth and let out a furious bellow.

"Callie, are you there?"

"Still here, Suzanne." Callie stuck a finger in her other ear in a futile attempt to muffle the din.

"It's about the exams for school readiness and placement. As our newest kindergarten teacher, you've been assigned to take over the testing of the four- and five-year-olds. You know, to decide if they're more suited to Pre-K or kindergarten. Isn't it exciting?"

"Exciting," Callie repeated less than excited. What in the world was this all about? She didn't recall ever being told about any testing.

She pulled the phone cord as far as it would extend and offered Danny a cookie. Valerie would have a fit, but right now she was more concerned with keeping him from disturbing Julian than worrying about the kid's glucose level. He stopped crying and eyed the cookie. In a flash, his plump little hand darted out to snatch the unexpected treat. He shoved it into his mouth.

Suzanne cleared her throat. "There's only one teeny problem."

"One teeny problem, you say? What's that?" Callie asked in a distracted voice, glancing at Danny. He grinned at her toothlessly and lobbed his gummed cookie across the room. It hit the bucket of soapy water with amazing accuracy. Danny shrieked with laughter. Well, Callie thought, it was better than tears.

"Mrs. Martin, our special-ed instructor, will be in Europe for the summer. Normally she'd test the new students for her department, but..." Suzanne gave a little laugh. "She can't if she's off gallivanting across the continent. So we thought of you, Callie. You'll be able to do it, won't you? Fill in for Mrs. Martin, I mean?''

This definitely violated Julian's third request. Not that she had much choice—not if she wanted her teaching job come September. "I guess I can," she agreed uneasily, then groaned, her attention caught by Danny's antics. Pleased by his success with the cookie, he tried the same thing with the pieces of his biscuit. Next went his bottle. It hit the linoleum and the cap dislodged, milk splattering everywhere. Her clean expanse of floor was rapidly taking on the appearance of a war zone.

"Super!" Suzanne exclaimed. "We'll let you know the exact dates sometime soon. Have to run. Don't forget about dropping off those cakes." The line went dead.

Julian's voice from behind her startled Callie. "What was all that about?" he wanted to know, watching as she bent to pick up the scattered bits of biscuit.

She shrugged. "Nothing important. The school needs some extra help with the placement testing for next year's students."

He grabbed her elbow and pulled her to her feet. "Forget the floor. I can do that. You sit and explain about this testing program."

Callie watched, blinking in surprise as Julian took a paper towel and dabbed at the soggy remnants of Danny's food barrage. Beneath his diligent attention, the mess grew steadily worse.

"Julian, why don't you let me—"

"No, no. I can handle it," he insisted. "So the school administrators decided you should do this testing? And naturally, you said yes. I thought we had an agreement. No more donating time or money until your present commitments are completed. Remember?"

"I remember. But this is different. This is work. The testing isn't just for them, Julian. It's for all the teachers and it's part of my job."

"Okay. I can accept that." He sat back on his heels and studied the tacky floor with satisfaction. "There. That should do it. What about Danny?" he continued. "I didn't notice him on your list."

She frowned. "That's because he's on the refrigerator. I mean Valerie's request is tacked there. Why are you so concerned with how I spend my time all of a sudden?"

He stood up. "You're a generous person, Callie. I sometimes think people take advantage of that generosity—to your detriment. The only way you're going to complete your current projects is if you don't take on any more. You also promised to give top priority to finding Maudie's will."

"Don't worry, the kids will help me with that. They should be along any minute." She grabbed the mop and worked it over the section of floor Julian had "cleaned."

He crossed to her side and took the mop away. "You're missing the point, Callie. If it didn't mean your possibly losing the house, I wouldn't give two hoots about finding that will. I'm just concerned about you wearing yourself out, trying to accomplish all these self-imposed tasks. I know you're still grieving for Maudie. But running yourself ragged isn't the best way to handle it."

Callie snatched the mop from his hands and thrust it back into the bucket. "And I think keeping busy is the best way to handle it. What about you? I heard you at your computer last night. You were working into the wee hours on that book, weren't you? Or is that different somehow?"

He shrugged. "Yes, it is different somehow. I've only taken on what I can handle. Can you say the same?"

"No," she admitted ruefully. "But then, I've never been able to claim that."

The back door opened and Donna and Cory walked in.

"Hi, Mr. Lord...Julian," Donna called out with a sunny grin, her neon hair now sporting green glitter.

Julian's eyebrows shot upward. "Hello," he greeted Donna cautiously before turning back to Callie. "I'll be upstairs in my temporary office, if you need me. Don't consider this discussion ended—just postponed. I hope you have a...productive day."

"You, too," Callie answered. Whether he knew it or not, their discussion was at a definite end. She turned to Cory. "Is your brother coming?"

"Sure is. He's really looking forward to getting his hands on this place. So what's on tap for us? More smash and crash?"

Callie laughed and shook her head. "How about a treasure hunt?" At their exclamations of delight, she explained Julian's plan. "I have no idea where to tell you to look for this note," she concluded. "It could be almost anywhere. All I ask is that you try and keep the volume down for Julian's sake."

She shook her head in amusement as the two set off in noisy confusion. She lifted Danny out of his high chair. "Well, what do you say, young man? Shall we skip the floor and take care of our errands? Suzanne said noon, and at the rate we're going it'll be that before we get out of here." The doorbell rang and she chuckled. "See what I mean?"

Callie hurried to the front of the house and opened the door to Cory's brother, Ted. She stared at him in dismay. He didn't appear to be any older than her high-school helpers, and he looked twice as disreputable. His clothes were fashionably ripped and he'd tied his long hair at the nape of his neck with a shoelace. Through a tear in his shirt she could make out a tatooed skull and crossbones.

He stepped over the threshold, looked around, then whistled.

"What a place." He skirted her, peering up and down the hallway. "Don't mind me," he said, as he pushed open the dining-room door. "Will ya look at this antique wiring? Old tube and knob. What a gas! I can't wait to have a go at it."

Callie's eyes widened in alarm. "Listen, Ted," she said quickly. "Mr. Lord wanted me to check with him before we did anything more with the house. I think he's worried about permits and . . . and plans and blueprints . . . all that stuff."

"Don't know anything about plans and blueprints, but you tell Mr. Lord I know my stuff just fine. Wait till he sees my bill."

"Bill?" Callie echoed in alarm. That meant money—something in painfully short supply these days. "Cory seemed to think we could reach some sort of agreement."

"Sure we can. You hand over lots of green paper and I fix your wires." He let out a whooping laugh and Danny burst into tears. Ted backed away, eyeing the baby with suspicion. "Listen, I'm going to have to check things out. You don't mind if I wander around, do you?"

"Well I—"

"Great." He headed for the hallway. "I didn't know they still had places like this standing. They've usually burned down long before now."

Callie nibbled on her lip. Maybe she should discuss this with Julian. He had made quite a point about the importance of checking with him before working on the house. But that would mean interrupting him. And yesterday on the raft he'd seemed very concerned about getting some time in on that book. Besides, Ted was just going to look around, not work. It wasn't as if he could do any real harm. That decided, she headed for the kitchen.

"Let's get those cakes to Suzanne," she said to Danny. "We'll deal with Ted later."

CALLIE RETURNED HOME in the middle of the afternoon. Delivering the cakes and other goodies had taken her longer than she'd anticipated. Upon her arrival at the Hankum farm, she'd discovered that Suzanne had called with instructions to pick up several more donations. By the time she'd finished running around half of Willow and dropping Danny back at Valerie's, she felt a bit frazzled.

She walked into the house, aware of excited voices coming from the library. Donna poked her head out.

"Come quick! We've found something!"

Callie hurried into the library. Cory and Donna stood with their heads together, studying a small envelope. Even Brutus had joined them, whining and shoving his way in between. Callie looked around the room at the stacks and stacks of books covering the floor.

"What in the world—" she began, only to be interrupted by Cory.

"We pulled everything off the shelves," he said, stating the obvious. "And look what we found." Triumphantly, he held out a small pink envelope.

"That's wonderful, Cory. It looks like another of Maudie's notes." She took the envelope and studied it. Her name and Julian's were scrawled on the front. "Maybe we should wait for Mr. Lord since it's addressed to him, too." At their groans of disappointment, she relented. "All right, let's see whether it's anything important. I wouldn't want to disturb him over a false alarm."

Feeling nervous, Callie broke the seal on the envelope and opened it. Inside was a slip of pale pink notepaper. She pulled it out and a light floral scent—Maudie's perfume—

wafted into the air. Callie blinked rapidly, fighting back a wave of grief, and forced herself to read the note.

Dear Callie and Julian,
Sorry. This note is not about the will. Don't give up, though! If you're reading this, it means I'm gone, so plant a flower in my memory. And when it blooms, remember how much I love you.

Aunt Maudie

By the time she'd finished the message, tears were streaming down her cheeks. Donna took one look and ran for the door, Brutus at her heels. Callie sat down on a small love seat and covered her face with her hands. How could Maudie think anyone would ever need a flower to remember her by? She lived in so many hearts, especially Callie's.

Hurried footsteps sounded on the stairs and Julian burst through the door. He spared one incredulous look around, then ordered sternly, "Out. Everyone out."

Once the room cleared, Julian sat down beside Callie. Gently he tilted her face and brushed the tears from her cheeks. "What is it, sweetheart?" he murmured. "What's happened?"

Without a word, she offered him Maudie's note. He tucked one arm around her shoulders, before taking the sheet of paper and reading it. "Damn," he muttered. His lips brushed the top of her head. "Don't cry, Callie. It's all right. We'll do it together, you and I. How about planting roses? She always loved roses."

Callie nodded, wiping her eyes. "Yellow Peace roses and pink Doloreses. And those big red ones with the heavy scent. She was crazy about them. We'll fill up the whole yard with roses so we can think about her all the time. We'll—"

A small sizzling sound distracted her. "What...?" Julian began just as the lights dimmed and went out. His body stiffened against hers. "Son of a..." he swore beneath his breath.

"Ted!" Callie whispered in dismay. "I should have known."

A moment later an incredible surge of power shot through the lines and the light bulbs flared so brightly Callie thought they'd explode.

"You realize this can't be happening," Julian remarked in a conversational tone. "I'm imagining this. I have to be."

Callie cleared her throat. "I'm afraid you aren't," she said as a loud pop resounded through the house. Then everything, the lights and all the electrical, went dead.

"Someone just killed my computer," came Julian's voice out of the darkness. "Fried its little electronic brains out, I'll bet. They hang people for less than that, don't they?"

CHAPTER SIX

Rule #10:
Mistakes happen.
Usually to those without a plan.

JULIAN SAT BEHIND THE DESK in his temporary office and stared at his computer—the same one that took a nose dive to China. Lord, was it only yesterday? He shoved his papers to one side and grabbed the phone. Within minutes he'd reached Brad.

"What's wrong, old buddy? You sound frustrated," his partner said, an amused edge in his voice.

"I am frustrated! I've just finished checking my files. It's as bad as I warned you. I lost everything when that...that crazy kid decided to play Ben Franklin with the power lines. My computer's completely blown. Over a week's worth of work wiped out."

"I can't believe you didn't bring your surge protector. That's not like you." Brad paused. "Maybe I should take over the project. I always did have a soft spot for Willow's End."

"Forget it," Julian said. "You'd be a basket case within twenty-four hours. Brutus on his worst day would have you pinned to the mat before you got through the door. And that's with one paw tied behind his back."

"One paw tied... What's gotten into you, Julian? You talk like that animal's a real person or something. If he's a problem, get rid of him."

"Get rid of him? Are you nuts?" Julian pulled himself up short. Was he actually defending that horrible hound? He must be spending too much time around Callie.

"I'm not suggesting anything drastic," Brad said. "Just find another home for him—somewhere in, say, Alaska."

Julian tried to picture Callie's reaction to the news that he'd relocated Brutus to Alaska, and shook his head. No way on God's green earth would he put her through something like that. The mere thought of anyone intentionally hurting Callie made him see red.

"Drop dead, Brad," he stated in no uncertain terms.

"Okay, okay. It was just a suggestion. But I have to tell you, Julian, I'm worried about you. No surge protector, talking as though that dog is a real person. Sounds to me like you're losing it."

"Losing what?"

"If you have to ask, you're in worse shape than I thought." Brad chuckled. "Losing your grip, old man. Julian Lord, the guy who has corporate execs cowering in terror, the master of rules and regulations, Mister I've-got-a-system himself, can't seem to organize one puny girl, a crazed electrician and a mischievous imp dressed in a doggy suit."

Julian held the receiver in a white-knuckled grip. If he could reach through the phone and get his hands around Brad's neck, one of them would die a happy man. And it wouldn't be his partner.

Brad laughed with an irreverent disregard for life and limb. "From what you say, there's an even chance you'll inherit Maudie's place. I really do love Willow's End—the lake, all that peace and quiet, that huge old house. Why don't you sell it to me and be done with it—before the old Julian goes down the tubes altogether."

"You need Willow's End about as much as a lobotomy," Julian snarled. "Though come to think of it..."

"Ah, come on, Julian," his partner wheedled. "Promise me if you inherit, you'll give me right of first refusal."

"Sure, Brad. Anything you say, Brad. You want the moon on a string? You got it. Just get off my back. Now what's the status on those seminars for Comptec? I need some updates."

"All right! That sounds more like the old—" Brad's voice came to an abrupt end.

Julian hit the cradle half a dozen times before he realized the line was dead. Dead as the proverbial doornail. He hung up the phone and his eyes narrowed in suspicion. It couldn't be. After that catastrophe yesterday, surely not even Callie's so-called electrician would have the nerve to return again today. Not if he knew what was good for him. With determined footsteps, Julian strode from the room. Enough was enough.

CALLIE TRIED to conceal her panic beneath a calm facade. "Can't you glue it back together?"

"That's supposed to be a joke, right?" Ted said.

"No. It isn't a joke. I'm very serious," she explained with care. "You're the electrical expert. You cut the line. You sew it up or . . . or tie it off. Just fix it. Fast."

"What're ya, nutty? Yeah, I know electric. But this ain't electric. It's a phone line. And I'm no Alexander Graham Bell. Try calling the phone company, why don'tcha."

"I *can't* call the phone company!" It took every ounce of control not to scream. "How am I supposed to get through? My phone's out of order because you cut the line. Remember?"

"Oh, yeah, that's right." His laugh reminded Callie of a donkey she'd once heard at the state fair. "Call the phone company, I tell her. Just dial 0 for operator. Whatta riot. That's one on me, I gotta admit. Walked right into—" Ted broke off, staring over her shoulder. He gave a queer sort of gulp, his face turning a pasty white.

Callie turned around, never doubting for a minute she'd see Julian. "Wonderful," she muttered, dredging up a weak smile. "You'd better come up with something good, Ted. And fast. This man has death written all over him."

Ted started to edge toward the door, talking fast. "Well, I'm outta here. Good luck with your phones, Callie. And with your electrical, too." That said, he took off, his tool belt jingling wildly about his hips.

"Hey, wait a minute!" she shouted after him. "You can't leave. What about my phone line? Ted!"

Julian came up behind her. "I'll kill him!" he stated, livid with rage. "No. First I'll kill you for letting him on the premises, and then I'll kill him. Either way, you're both dead."

"He—I—we—" She took a hasty step backward as his fury turned on her.

Callie didn't think she'd ever seen Julian quite so angry. Dark color swept across his cheeks and forehead, and he held his mouth in taut uncompromising lines. She forced herself to meet his eyes. They weren't brown anymore. Not one speck of chocolate remained to tempt her in those hard black eyes.

"How could you?" he demanded, towering over her. "How could you let him come back after what he did yesterday? Don't your promises mean anything to you?"

"Of course they do." She inched away, attempting to explain. "Ted wanted to help. He felt so awful about your computer. He begged me to let him make amends. What could I do?"

It was the wrong question to ask.

Julian stepped closer, his voice raspy and dangerously soft. "What could you do? Try saying no! It's simple— honest it is. No. Two little letters. Try it. No."

"Julian—"

"Not Julian. No. The word is no."

"You don't understand."

He ran a hand through his hair. "You can't say it, can you? That's why you spend your entire life taking on everyone else's jobs and chores and responsibilities. The whole town of Willow knows it. Good old Callie, always ready, willing and able... to play the patsy."

She felt the color drain from her face and couldn't hide the hurt his words inflicted. He was being unfair. She only tried to live by the Golden Rule. Was that so wrong? She'd always thought it admirable, yet Julian seemed to consider it a flaw.

Callie gathered her dignity around her like a cloak and looked up at him. "I try to help people, Julian. It's what I like to do. If that's wrong, then I'm sorry, though I never thought it was something I should apologize for."

Julian grimaced. "Perhaps I've stated this more strongly than necessary. Helping others is fine, Callie, and it's nice to be needed. But you take it too far. You must admit, the results have been less than perfect."

"You mean Ted."

His gaze sharpened. "I mean Ted, the repairs, Danny, and all the other various and sundry projects you have going. Callie, we started to discuss this once before and we never got to finish the conversation. Perhaps we should."

She shook her head, feeling wounded and defensive. "Perhaps we shouldn't. We're never going to agree on this. It's important for me to help others, whereas you think it's a nuisance. I don't see room for compromise, so I suggest we don't even try."

"I agree." Julian stared down at her, his expression hardening. "It also proves to me that selling this place may be our only option. I can't force you to give up Willow's

End should you inherit, but that choice has a strong appeal should I inherit the house."

"You can't mean that! You couldn't sell Willow's End and live with yourself afterward."

"Couldn't I? We'll have to wait and see, won't we? As things stand, I have no choice. The responsibility for this house has been dumped in my lap whether I like it or not. Well, we've tried things your way. It didn't work. Now we'll do things mine."

Callie felt a hint of unease. "What do you mean?"

"I mean that until we know who the rightful owner of Willow's End is, I'm taking over." He adjusted his glasses, intimidating her with his businesslike stance. "My computer's blown and the shop has no idea how long the repairs will take. If I can get this mess with the house and the will straightened out, I'll be able to get my book written the minute the computer's back up."

Callie didn't like the sound of that. "Maybe if you searched for the will, the kids and I could—"

"Forget it. Actually, these repairs may prove to be a blessing in disguise. It gives us a chance to look for the will while we get the house into a livable condition." He smiled without humor. "Have your crew here bright and early tomorrow morning. And by that I do not mean ten. I mean eight. I'll let you know then what your assignments will be."

"Oh, Julian," Callie groaned. "You're not going to start that first, second and third stuff again, are you?"

"If that's what it takes to get things done around here, then that's precisely what I'll do."

"WE'VE TRIED these past two weeks, Callie. Honestly we have," Cory said. "The problem is . . ."

Donna gave a wistful sigh. "He really is thirty, isn't he?"

"You've got that right," Cory agreed. "And look what he did to my poor brother. Ted went out and joined the navy just to avoid meeting up with Mr. Lord again."

Callie put her hands on her hips. "Don't exaggerate—"

"Who's exaggerating? My mom's thrilled to pieces. It's the first time in five years all the lights have worked." He grinned. "She wants to thank the old guy by baking him a pie."

Callie stared at him. "The old guy? I hope you don't mean Mr. Lord."

Donna interrupted. "Forget the pie, Cory. And forget your stupid brother, too. No one cares about any of that. What we do care about is this business with the lists." She looked meaningfully at Cory, satisfied when he gave her an emphatic nod of agreement. "It's time to get serious. We need to decide what we're going to do."

"What you're going to do is get to work," Callie stated in a no-nonsense voice.

" 'Fraid not." Cory sat down on the kitchen floor and folded his arms across his chest. "Consider this a mutiny. You know, a sit-out. Like they used to do in the olden days."

"A sit-out? You mean a sit-in? But this isn't—" the time for a history lesson, she realized, as Donna joined Cory on the floor. Callie studied their frowns of displeasure with growing alarm.

She had to find some way to change their minds. Because if she didn't, the pair would find themselves right back at juvey hall answering to a judge who wouldn't look too kindly on this latest incident. It also meant she'd fail to complete Maudie's final request—a request she'd avoided mentioning to Julian. Worst of all, she'd fail these kids and they could suffer the consequences of today's impulsive action for the rest of their lives. For their sakes, she had to prevent that from happening.

"I know this isn't what you're used to and that the changes have been a bit drastic. But I wish you'd give Julian another chance," Callie pleaded. She held up her hands at the clamorous protests. "Give it one more day, that's all I'm asking. You've made it through these past two weeks. Can't you live through one more day?"

"Highly doubtful," Cory replied. "I mean, we're talking major attitude adjustment here. That's asking an awful lot, you know?"

Callie thought fast, knowing she'd hate herself later for what she was about to do. "Fine. Five bucks a day—each— for a major attitude adjustment. Take it or leave it."

"Ten and you've got a deal," Donna shot back.

Twenty dollars. It would put a big dent in tomorrow's paycheck, but it was worth it. "Okay. But that means you keep his schedule to the millisecond if that's what he wants. And Cory—" she glared at the main offender "—no more smart remarks. Another crack about having to send out messages by smoke signals because the phone's still not working, and the deal's off. Are we agreed?"

"Agreed," the two chorused enthusiastically.

Callie spent the rest of the day riddled with guilt for having bribed the kids. The added discovery that the bribe was unnecessary only intensified her dismay. The minute Julian came downstairs, it was clear he'd changed. Gone was the business executive with his lists and detailed instructions. In his place stood a cheerful energizing leader who, within minutes, had her helpers climbing all over themselves to do his bidding.

For a while Callie tried to contribute, but gradually she drifted to the fringes of the group, dismayed by the strange emotions gripping her. She slumped to the floor, feeling ignored and left out of their enchanted circle. They didn't seem to need her and she didn't like the feeling, not one little bit.

As though aware of her distress, Brutus lumbered into the room and sat down beside her. He gave her face a comforting lick. With a sigh she wrapped her arms about his neck, wishing his brandy cask contained real brandy. She'd have to correct that oversight one of these days.

"Okay, you two. That's it for now." Julian called a halt to the day's activities late that afternoon. "You've worked very hard the past couple of weeks and I appreciate it. This place is really shaping up. A few more weeks and we'll have all our walls back."

"Too bad we haven't found the will," said Cory. "I suppose three socks, two of Maudie's 'it's not here' notes and a pair of bloomers isn't such a bad haul."

"Not bad at all. Though proper wiring, real walls and a coat of paint would be even better," Julian said. "Now that the house is approaching a livable state, we'll concentrate on finding that will. In the meantime, I want to thank you for all you've done. I've arranged for free banana splits at Farkle's Ice Cream Parlor." He grinned. "Just be sure you're not too stuffed to come back here for a swim."

In the resulting din, Callie buried her face in Brutus's coat. "That's just great!" she muttered. "Ruin their teeth. Load them up on sugar. And using bribery, of all things. How low can you get?"

"Fantastic!" Cory exclaimed. "Twenty bucks from Callie to end our sit-out, *plus* free splits from Mr. Lord. That's what I call an outstanding day."

The silence that followed their noisy exit was positively deafening. "Buying them off?" Julian cross-examined her, moving his stepladder to the middle of the study. "I'm surprised at you, Callie." He climbed up to inspect the ceiling, appearing satisfied with the final paint job.

"What do you call banana splits at Farkle's?" she demanded. "A pat on the head?"

"In a way, yes. They gave their all the past couple of weeks and I wanted to show my gratitude." He sat down on the top step and studied her, his gaze cool and a touch reproving. "But bribery..." He shook his head. "You blew it, second cuz."

Julian was right, Callie admitted to herself. She shouldn't have bribed them. But she'd been desperate. What else could she have done? She inched closer to Brutus, struggling to gather her courage to apologize. "So I'm human," she muttered without thinking into the dog's ear. "Julian would be human, too—if someone knocked him down to earth to join the rest of us mere mortals."

With a happy bark, Brutus lunged to his feet and barreled toward the ladder.

"No, wait!" she called, an instant too late. "I didn't mean it!"

At Callie's cry of warning, Brutus made a gallant effort to stop in time. He backpedaled frantically—to no avail. His huge body spun sideways and his tail and hip hit the ladder dead-on, sweeping it out from under Julian.

The ladder crashed to the ground, taking Julian along with it.

Callie covered her eyes, cringing at the noise. A long silent minute ticked by before she got up the nerve to peek through her fingers. She winced. Her stepbrother lay sprawled on the floor with Brutus collapsed at his side.

Julian lifted his head and looked at the dog. "*Et tu, Brute,*" he said. Then, with a groan, his head fell back and he closed his eyes.

Callie jumped to her feet and rushed to him. "Julian! Julian, are you all right?" She knelt on the floor, staring down at his pale still face and caught her breath in alarm. "Oh, no! Please don't be hurt. I'm sorry. I didn't mean it. I never meant for Brutus to really do it."

A horrible thought struck her. What if Julian had broken something in the fall? What if he'd hit his head and was in a coma? "I can't remember what you do for head wounds," she moaned. "Is it feet up or head up?"

Brutus settled the issue for her. He stuck his nose against Julian's and gave him a lick.

"Cut that out!" Julian blasted, his eyes still closed. "You've done enough damage without slobbering all over me."

Callie gave a little gasp of relief. "Julian?"

One eyelid lifted. "Who the hell else would it be?" he snarled and shut his eye again.

"Um, are you all right?" she asked. "You're not moving."

"Hey, I'm no fool. I move and that spawn of Hades eats me."

She blinked in bewilderment. "Who? Brutus? Why would he eat you?"

"Why does he do anything he does? Because he's insane." Julian folded his arms across his chest. "I'm not taking any chances. I'll stay right here, thank you all the same."

"He only knocked you off the ladder because I told him to," Callie explained apologetically. "He won't eat you unless I say so, and I won't. I promise."

"That makes me feel much much better. You make a habit of this sort of thing?"

"Yes. Yes, I do," she confessed, guilt overriding all other emotions. "Oh, why can't I stop and think, instead of saying the first thing that pops into my head?" She glared at Brutus. "And darn it all! Why do you have to take everything I say so literally? I said *someone*. Do you know the word someone? Someone should knock him off the ladder. Not *you*. *Someone* should push Gwen in the lake. Get it? Someone does not mean you!"

Brutus gave a sharp bark in response.

"Gwen?" Julian opened his eyes to glance from Callie to the dog. "Let me take a wild guess here."

Brutus shook his head and let out a pathetic whine. As though to make amends, he tried to climb onto Julian's lap.

The breath whooshed out of Julian's lungs. "Cut that out or you'll kill me for sure," he managed to say, pushing at the huge animal. "Go on now, sit down. I'm not mad at you." Julian's gimlet stare came to rest on Callie. "You, on the other hand, are a different story."

"I can explain," she stated in a rush.

"I'll bet. Start with Gwen and move forward from there."

"Gwen. Right." She twisted her fingers together. "You see, we were out by the lake and Gwen said some things that I didn't quite... quite..."

"Quite like?" Julian tossed out.

"Like." Callie leapt at the word as eagerly as a fish at a lure. "Good. I didn't quite *like* her topic of conversation and as a result I sort of lost my temper. I said that *some-one*—" she paused long enough to glare at Brutus again "—should push her in the lake."

"And?"

She gulped. "And someone did. Afterward Gwen claimed I was responsible."

"I know." His voice had an angry inflection.

Callie stirred uneasily, wondering whether his ire was directed at her or at Gwen. Either way, it didn't matter. Gwen hadn't been in the wrong—a fact that needed to be made clear to him.

"It was all my fault," Callie insisted earnestly. "I may not have pushed her in the lake with my own two hands, but I was responsible. Which is why I accepted the blame..."

Julian sat up and groaned, holding a hand to his ribs. "You don't need to tell me any more. I get the picture." His dark eyes, when they met hers, no longer looked angry. Instead there seemed to be a hint of amusement in the rich brown depths.

"I've always known that Brutus knocked Gwen in the lake," he said. "My bedroom window faces in that direction. I saw the whole thing. I just didn't realize you ordered Brutus to, er, carry out the execution. And until today, I wouldn't have believed it even if you had told me."

"Because you didn't think Brutus understood." It was a statement, rather than a question. A tiny smile curved her lips. "I assume you believe it now?"

"Let's say I'm willing to be a bit more broad-minded about that possibility." He reached out and gave her long brown hair a gentle tug. "You blamed yourself for my breakup with Gwen, didn't you, green eyes?" At Callie's nod, his expression turned serious. "Our relationship ended the moment she lied about you."

"Oh," Callie said weakly. "I wish I'd known."

"Try asking next time." He studied her, curiosity reflected in his voice. "I know what I said *now* to make you so mad. What horrible thing did Gwen say *then* that rated a dunking?"

His question caught her by surprise, and brilliant color flooded Callie's face. No way would she answer that one, she decided. Her lips were sealed, taped and locked shut. Not under pain of death would she tell him what Gwen had said to her. It was too humiliating. Retreat seemed the best option. With more haste than grace, she attempted to scramble to her feet.

"Oh, no, you don't!" Julian's hand shot out and encircled her wrist. "You're not going anywhere until we finish this conversation. Spill it." With apparent ease, he pulled her to his side.

"No!"

"You owe me that much, Callie. In fact, it's the very least you owe me. Give. What did she say?"

Callie attempted to palm him off with a nonanswer. "She was rude. And if there's anything I can't stand it's rude people." She gave an experimental tug of her arm. His grip, though light, would not be easily broken.

"Bull. Tell me the real reason."

Callie licked her lips, looking everywhere but at Julian. Why wasn't Brutus helping her? Why did he just sit there with that stupid grin on his face?

She couldn't tell Julian the truth. He'd get the wrong idea. Or worse, he'd get the right idea. He'd think she—

"Callie!"

"Gwen told me I was in love with you," she blurted, responding to the sharp command in his voice. She groaned inwardly. So much for seals, tape and locks. So much for pain of death. Telling him the truth was worse than any death. She sighed. "Gwen said I was making cow eyes at you, and if I didn't cut it out she'd...she'd..."

"She'd what?" he prompted quietly.

"She said she'd tell you and Maudie." Callie bowed her head, her words whisper-soft. "She said it was wrong for me to feel anything but brotherly affection for you."

There was a moment of silence and Callie couldn't resist a quick peek upward. Her heart began to pound. Watching Julian's sudden grasp of the situation was like watching a light come on. She could almost see him replaying the events of the past several weeks in his mind, see him turning them over, analyzing them and realizing at last what they meant.

His eyes darkened to ebony and shone with a strange gleam.

Feeling brutally exposed by her admission, she waited in dread for him to laugh, or worse, pity her. But the teasing remarks she half expected never came. To her surprise, a warm lazy smile spread across Julian's mouth. She inhaled, recognizing the ardent glow of desire in his gaze. It did peculiar things to her breathing.

Julian spoke in a rough-edged voice. "You didn't feel brotherly affection for me then, did you? Any more than you feel that way now."

He didn't wait for a response, which was fortunate, since she had none to give. His hand left her wrist and moved up the length of her arm in teasing little circles. "What if I told you that I'm not interested in brotherly affection?" he murmured. "What if I said that my present feelings for you bear no relationship to how brothers or sisters or even second cousins, twice removed, feel?"

Callie trembled beneath his wandering fingers, struggling to think straight. She didn't dare read more into his statement than the words themselves. Hadn't she made that mistake before? Of course he didn't feel like a relative. He wasn't one. They'd been briefly related through an accident of marriage—with *accident* being the predominant word.

His hand reached her shoulder and started down again, the volatile touch causing lightninglike prickles to dance across her skin. She forced back a moan. She had to keep her head. She couldn't let her guard down for even an instant. If she did...

"Talk to me, Callie. Don't be shy." The way he spoke her name did strange and wonderful things to her equilibrium. "What if I told you that I'm attracted to you? What would you say then?"

She shook her head. He didn't mean it. He couldn't mean it. Yet the hint of passion deepening his voice told a different story. His hand traced her jawline and a minute shiver shook her. Nervously she licked her dry lips.

It never failed. All he had to do was touch her, and she was helpless. Totally helpless. She wanted so much to believe him, to give in to her natural inclinations. But she wouldn't make a fool of herself again. This time he'd have to say what he felt—and in words that couldn't be mistaken.

"You say 'what if,' Julian." She struggled to sound cool and detached. "What ifs are just fantasies. They're pleasant to dream about, but they're not real." Her eyes met his and she became lost in their dark velvet depths. Perhaps she'd settle for fantasies, after all, if it meant sharing them with Julian.

He took off his glasses. His expression was serious, his face carved into lines of determination. Something else was reflected there, as well, something she found more difficult to understand, something beyond her realm of experience.

"This *is* real, Callie, not a fantasy." Julian leaned toward her and cupped her face with both his hands, his breath mingling with hers. "What I'm feeling, right this instant, is as real as you and me." His intense gaze held her. "Can you deny it?"

Any doubts she might have had were thrust to one side. "No."

The word trembled between them, and Julian whispered her name. Then there were no words, only sensation as he pulled her into his arms.

Julian didn't immediately kiss her. His mouth hovered over hers until she felt him with every nerve. Just when she thought she couldn't bear another moment without his touch, his hard mouth covered hers. Callie slid her arms around his neck, her lips parting beneath his, giving to him with all her heart.

She loved him, she realized in that instant. For more than a year she'd tried to deceive herself, but no more. She wouldn't hide from her newfound knowledge any longer.

Whatever Julian's true feelings for her, she was now committed to him.

Gradually he eased their embrace, his hand trailing slowly down her back. "This wasn't what I'd planned," he murmured.

Callie sighed, burying her face against his throat. "Does everything with you have to be planned?"

Julian chuckled. "No. Our first kiss, the one on the raft, wasn't planned, was it?" At her noncommittal shrug, he pressed, "As I recall, that one was every bit as spontaneous as this."

"Maybe so," she admitted reluctantly, pulling back so she could meet his eyes. "But that kiss doesn't count." When his eyebrows shot up in astonishment, she felt obligated to explain. "It wasn't a real one. You were still my brother, then."

Julian burst out laughing. "You've got a thing or two to learn about brotherly kisses, sweetheart." He slid his hands into her hair and pulled her face to within inches of his. "But you won't learn them from me."

"No?" Callie whispered.

"No. And since the first one didn't count, here's another kiss to make up for it."

"Another kiss to make up for what?" Cory demanded from the dining-room door. "What's going on? What did we miss?" He turned to yell down the hall. "You're missing something good in here, Donna. They're talking about kissing and stuff."

"I'll be talking about death and *stuff* if you don't get your nosy little face out of this room!" Julian said in his most quelling tone.

Not that it was sufficient to quell Cory. He grinned engagingly. "Hey, don't mind me. I just wanted to let Callie know that we voted and it's unanimous."

Callie could only stare at him, lost. "Voted?" she repeated, feeling flushed and self-conscious. "About what?"

"You know. About working for Mr. Lord and you paying us. We decided you could forget about the sit-out money. Today has been so decent, it wouldn't be right. We'll be down by the lake if you need us for anything." His grin turned to a leer. "I guess you can go back to what you were doing before I came in. *I* sure would!"

With that, he ducked his head out of the doorway. The only sound in the room was the echo of his footsteps as he pelted down the hall.

Julian sat up and put on his glasses. "You don't have to increase their wages. I know they were on the verge of rebellion over the change in work habits I'd instituted. But we'd have come to an agreement eventually."

"Do you think so?" she responded, noting his change in mood with regret. "I'm sorry, Julian. It seemed the only way to keep them working."

He lifted his eyebrows. "By using bribery? As a schoolteacher, you should know better than that."

Callie sighed. "Perhaps I could have handled it differently. But I'm not sure how. They came to me. They were upset. They were just about to quit and I didn't want that to happen. So I—"

"Bribed them. I shouldn't have to explain the flaw in that reasoning to you." He eyed her sternly. "But I will. First, bribery never works. All it does is teach greed."

"Farkle's wasn't a bribe?"

He shook his head. "No. It wasn't. Showing your appreciation for services rendered is not the same as paying people off so they'll work in the first place."

Callie thought about it, then nodded. After all, he was right. "Okay. I see your point."

"Good. Second. If they'd been working for anyone else and tried this stunt, they'd have been fired on the spot.

What you should have done was—" he ticked the points off on his fingers "—have them sit down and draft out a list of their complaints and demands. Come to me and present their grievances in a well-thought-out adult manner. Learn to compromise when, ultimately, I didn't give in to all their requests."

It was so simple Callie couldn't believe she hadn't thought of it first. Desperation did strange things to a person. She sighed and offered him a wry smile. "Should I grovel yet, or do you have a third point to make?"

His lips twitched. "Save the grovel. It may come in handy later. In the meantime...third. I have a rule that I use in business. It's my number-one rule and goes, 'Never be so dependent on something you'll do anything to keep it.'" His expression turned serious. "I believe you compromise your values otherwise. That rule also pertains to people. What if Cory and Donna had become bored with the whole project? What would you have done then?"

"I don't know," Callie confessed. She didn't like the sound of his number-one rule. It made her uneasy. Did his determination never to be dependent on anything apply to his feelings for her, too? Could this be a subtle warning?

"If they'd become bored, you'd have gotten someone else, someone better suited to the job," he told her a shade impatiently.

Gotten someone else? Did he think everyone and everything was replaceable? Callie lifted her chin. "No, I wouldn't, because Cory and Donna *have* to work for me. It's that, or—"

Oops. She slanted him a swift guilty look, seeing his eyes narrow in sudden suspicion. Looked like confession time had arrived. Honesty is the best policy, Maudie always said. Best she followed Maudie's policy before he killed her. Callie cleared her throat. "Uh, there might be one tiny little detail I overlooked mentioning."

"Just one tiny little detail?" Julian repeated dryly.

"Just one." She twisted her fingers together. "It's about Maudie's third request."

His eyebrows shot upward. "Maudie's *third* request?"

"Right." She smiled brightly. "The one that has to do with Cory and Donna and their being on probation. That one detail."

CHAPTER SEVEN

Rule #41:
*Habits are like fleas on a dog.
You can scratch,
but real relief only comes with flea powder.*

"EXPLAIN, AND FAST!" Julian ordered.

Callie swallowed. "Cory and Donna got in a little bit of trouble with the law. Maudie heard about it and agreed to oversee their probation time. So the judge ordered them to perform community service hours by working at Willow's End." She ground to a halt and waited for the explosion. It wasn't long in coming.

Dark red color climbed from his jawline. "You know damned well you overlooked mentioning that *one tiny little detail!* The truth is, you were very careful *not* to mention Maudie's third request. And I have a pretty good idea why. You knew I'd never agree to it!"

She didn't bother to deny the truth of his statement. "I didn't have a choice!" she said instead. "I couldn't refuse Maudie. She was dying!"

He took a deep breath, struggling to control his temper. "I can sympathize with your predicament, but damn it Callie!" He paced the floor in front of her. "How long is this probation to last? What are they in for?"

"It's only for the summer," she temporized.

He pinned her with his gaze. "And their crime?"

"Destruction of property," she muttered.

"Destruction of property!" She thought he'd blow a gasket. "You're rehabilitating these two for destruction of property by having them rip apart Willow's End? Is it just me, or is there something wrong with this picture?"

"You're not going to take this well, are you?"

"You've got that right." He gave a sharp laugh. "What is it with you? Where's your sense of responsibility?"

"Right where it should be," she flashed back. "Helping people in need—"

"And taking on the entire world's problems, regardless of whether or not you can cope. Not that generosity is a bad quality, but you can take a good thing too far. In fact, you're an expert at taking good things too far."

"If that's supposed to be an insult, you'll have to try harder," she informed him. "I explained about Maudie's requests. I just ... forgot to tell you about the third one."

"Convenient memory you have there." He thrust a hand through his hair. "What should I do, Callie, stand idly by while you drive yourself into the ground? I can't do that. If you keep overextending yourself, you're going to crash. And I don't want to be the one left picking up the pieces. Not if I can prevent it from happening—by selling the house."

"I wish you'd stop threatening to sell Willow's End," she retorted. "The house has nothing to do with my wanting to help people."

He turned on her. "Why do you do it?"

"What?"

"Not what. Why. Why do you like helping others?" He didn't give her a chance to respond. "It's because you need to be needed. I'm willing to bet we have Helene to thank for that."

"My mother has nothing to do with it!"

"Hit too close to home, did I?" He approached her, following as she backed away. "It explains a lot, when you think about it. A mother who abandons you, who moves discontentedly from place to place and husband to husband, always looking for the perfect life and the perfect love. And overlooking it in the one place it's always been—with her daughter.''

"No," Callie said, shaking her head. "You're wrong."

He stepped closer, until her back was against the wall and she had no place to run. "A daughter who learns to give and give and give, in the hope of getting a shred of that love and attention that's always been withheld. Think about it, Callie."

She glared at him. "No, thanks. That has nothing to do with anything. I never would have bribed those kids in the first place if it hadn't been for your lists and schedules."

He braced his hands on the wall on either side of her head. "Changing the subject? Good try, but it won't wash. You're grasping at straws."

She lifted her chin. Changing the subject and grasping at straws were both time-honored practices. "My helping people isn't nearly as bad as your stupid timetables. You don't make a move unless it's planned. Next you'll be slotting me into your daily diary. You know—'8:01 a.m. to 8:05 a.m.: kiss Callie.'''

"Sounds great to me." He bent his head, his mouth inches from hers. "And just so you know, it's 4:56 p.m."

His lips covered hers and Callie sighed against his mouth, finding she couldn't think, much less argue. Her hands crept up along his chest to his shoulders. For so long she'd dreamed of this, imagined what it would be like to be held by him, kissed and caressed by him. Now she knew. No dream could match the reality of it. The wonder of it.

His hand slid up from her waist, grazing her breast, and she caught her breath. The sensations chasing through her were unlike any she'd ever experienced. As though his thoughts and feelings echoed hers, he shuddered against her.

Gradually his hold eased and he lifted his head to stare down at her, his gaze dark and impassioned. "Well?" he demanded. "Was that spontaneous enough for you?"

"Okay," she gasped, more dazed than she cared to admit. "So you don't plan everything. But you'll never convince me you can live without your lists and schedules."

"Think not? There's one way we can find out."

"Which is?"

His eyes gleamed. "Care to make a small wager?"

"Another bet!" Callie exclaimed, laughing. "I love it—it's the perfect solution. I'll bet you can't go for one week without a watch, clock, timetable or list."

Julian lowered his head, his lips nuzzling the sensitive area just below her ear. "What about my schedules?"

She fought to speak normally. "It's all the same thing."

Julian chuckled and released her, allowing her to breathe more freely. "Wait a minute. Don't you want to hear what you'll have to do? You might not be willing to go through with it once you know."

She fell silent, studying him suspiciously. "What is it?"

His smile made her nervous. "To win the bet, you have to say no to any and all favors—for one week."

Callie nibbled her lower lip. "Any and all favors. Just what does that mean?"

"Precisely what it says. When Suzie Whatsit calls up with some new school project, you have to say no. When Valerie calls up desperate for a baby-sitter for dear Danny, the answer is no."

"That's it?" She gave him a cheeky grin. "It'll be a snap. I'll just have Ted come back and cut the phone lines again."

"Over my dead body."

"More like over his." She tilted her head to one side. "Why do I feel as if I've been very cleverly maneuvered?"

"Because you have been cleverly maneuvered, sweetheart," he flashed back.

Callie's eyes widened. She hadn't seen Julian so carefree in ages. A feeling of wonderment crept over her. Could she have done that for him? Was it possible?

"I'm hoping," he continued, "by taking a week off you'll discover how much you've been overdoing recently." Before she could argue the point, he added, "If you do manage to win, I'll help you complete Maudie's final two requests without complaint or interference."

She brightened. "Really? I like the sound of that. But what if I lose and you win?"

"The reverse. You do things my way."

"Without complaint or interference," she finished for him. And since his losing was practically a given, she permitted herself a pleased little smile.

He raised an eyebrow. "You don't think I can get by without my lists, do you?"

Callie shook her head. "No way."

"Very well, we'll see." He unstrapped his watch and handed it to her. "Here. Though I'll get it back soon enough. You can't go seven minutes, let alone seven days, without caving in and helping someone."

She made a face at him. "Which is about how long you can go without your precious lists."

He leaned toward her. "Then it's a bet?" At Callie's nod, he tugged her closer. "Why don't we seal it with a kiss?"

JULIAN JOINED CALLIE the next morning at breakfast. "Something's come up," he announced without preamble. Grim-faced, he poured himself a cup of black coffee. Then, to her intense pleasure, he tugged her out of her chair and took it himself, pulling her down on his lap.

He ran a gentle hand across her cheek. "You're not going to like it much."

His tone of voice worried her—it was serious, very serious, and rough, as though he fought some strong emotion. But his eyes gave away his intense anger. Deep in their rich darkness burned a fury that frightened her.

She rested a hand on his shoulder. "What's happened?" she demanded. "What's wrong?"

"My father phoned."

Normally that information wouldn't have been cause for concern. The very starkness of his words warned her otherwise. Her hand tightened on his shoulder. "What did he want?"

He stared down into his coffee mug, then lifted it and took a swallow of the scalding liquid. "Willow's End."

"I don't understand," Callie whispered. "What do you mean?"

His gaze slammed into her. "Yes, you do understand. I told you this could happen. I explained the urgency of finding that will. Jonathan's heard it's missing. I don't know where or how he got his information, but at this point, it doesn't matter. He knows. In two weeks he's coming back to claim Maudie's estate."

"Why? What does he want it for?"

Julian's lips twisted into a cynical smile. "He intends to do just what I said he'd do. He's going to sell it. His latest expedition is low on funds and he wants the money."

She struggled to control the surge of panic that gripped her. "No! That's not right. It's not fair."

She hated the expression in Julian's eyes. It told her all too clearly that what was right and fair wasn't worth a hill of beans. It was a harsh reality to face.

He held her in a close comforting embrace, his hand entangled in her hair. "We could chuck it all—forget the will, forget Willow's End." He rested his chin against the top of her head. "I've suddenly discovered something very special in the middle of all this chaos, and I don't have the time to savor it.''

His suggestion tempted her. It tempted her a lot. "Is that what you really want?" she asked tentatively. "To give up?"

He groaned. "No. As much as I want time alone with you, as much as I worry about your welfare, I can't forget my responsibilities so easily. It's Maudie's wishes that should determine who gets Willow's End, not my father's greed.''

''What should we do then?''

''We find that will. It's our only chance. We might be able to prove its existence, but not even Peters can testify as to what it says. He claims she changed it so many times he doesn't know how the final version read. And without the will, that's what's needed—someone to swear in court as to the contents.''

''Then we find the will,'' she said matter-of-factly. She reached for a piece of toast and dabbed some butter on it. ''We haven't been trying very hard. Now we will—must. Today when the kids arrive, we'll have another treasure hunt. We'll organize it so that every inch of Willow's End is covered.''

Julian laughed, the tension draining from his body. ''That's a lot of inches.''

She held the toast to his mouth. ''Then you'd better eat. You're going to need your strength.''

He took a quick bite. ''You've forgotten something.''

Callie looked at him, puzzled. ''What?''

His eyes held an endearing mischievous expression. ''Our bet started this morning. I can't organize anything.''

She scowled. ''That's nasty, Julian. Here we are in dire straits, and you're going on about that stupid bet. How petty can you get?''

"Pretty petty, my sweet." He snatched the final bit of toast from her hand. "I'll leave the organizing to you. It'll do you good. You take care of the lists and assignments and I'll—"

"You'll what?"

He planted a buttery kiss on her lips. "Why, I'll obey your every command, of course."

Callie sighed, snuggling deeper into his embrace. When he held her like this, kissed her, she could almost forget the threat of losing Willow's End. Almost.

CALLIE WAITED until everyone was seated at the dining-room table before going through the assignments she'd drawn up for the day. If the success of the project hadn't been so important, she'd have laughed at the bemused expressions on the young faces.

"Is this for real?" Cory demanded. "You're making up the lists now?"

"'Fraid so," Callie said. "We're running out of time. So please do your best. If you find any clue, no matter how insignificant, bring it to us." She handed Julian his sheet of paper. "You're in the attic. It's going to be a waste of time, but you said cover everything."

"Not to worry. Better we do this logically, top to bottom, than risk overlooking something."

"I suppose. It's just that Maudie *never* went up there. She hated it. It's dirty—"

"No problem."

"There's all these cobwebs."

"I can handle it."

"And the spiders—"

"Callie!"

She suppressed a smile. "All right, all right. But don't say I didn't warn you." She handed the next piece of paper to Cory. "You're in the library."

"Again?" He groaned. "We just got all those books put away. Have a heart."

"I do. And it's in this house." She gave Donna her list. "Notice that I jotted down a few suggestions about where to look. Be sure you check those areas in each of your assigned rooms. And remember, Maudie had a strange sense of humor, so use your imagination. I'll be searching the kitchen if you need me."

"Yes, boss." Cory snapped a salute and stood up. "We'll hop to it right away." He turned to leave the room, nudging Donna as he went. "They think Maudie was strange? She didn't have anything on these two."

The day seemed interminable. Callie pulled every last dish from the kitchen shelves. She examined every pot, canister and bowl, every box, appliance and cupboard, and found nothing except a bit of dust and an old dog biscuit.

Late in the afternoon Donna and Cory trailed into the kitchen. "Didn't find a thing," Cory told her with an apologetic shrug. "Maybe tomorrow."

"Right, maybe tomorrow," Callie agreed, struggling to sound optimistic. Long after they'd gone she continued to sit in the middle of the kitchen floor. Dishes and pans were piled around her, and looking at them, she considered bursting into tears. Not that it would help. It would just make her feel a whole lot better.

In need of some doggy comfort, she called to Brutus. When he lumbered close enough to hug, she threw her arms around him.

"Do you suppose Julian's had any success?" she asked. He shook his huge head and she sighed. "Well, it isn't like we're out of places to look. We'll run out of time long before we run out of rooms."

She'd been so certain the will would magically turn up. "Darn it, Maudie, where did you put that will?" Callie demanded out loud, struggling to her feet.

"That's one method of finding the thing that didn't occur to me," Julian said from directly behind her. "If she answers, let me know."

Callie turned around, her eyes widening. Dust and dirt covered him from head to toe. "Oh, my gosh."

"Come now. Can't you think of something stronger than that to say? How about 'Golly gee'?"

"Okay. Golly gee. Though I did warn you about the attic." She looked at him hopefully. "Did you find anything? Anything at all?"

Julian shook his head, spinning off a little cloud of dust. Brutus sneezed and Callie covered her mouth to hide a grin, amazed she could still laugh, considering the circumstances. Their situation wasn't the least bit funny. In fact, it was downright bleak.

"Come on upstairs. We can talk after I shower and change," Julian instructed. The three of them trooped to the second floor and he parked Callie in his office before striding through a connecting door to his bedroom.

Since Julian's return, she'd never dared set foot near his rooms. Now she looked around with interest. Neat piles of paper were stacked on his worktable and, curious, she studied them.

"Are all these rules?" she called out to him. "What do you need so many for?"

"They're for my time-management book. Read them. You might find one or two useful."

She frowned at his dreaded first rule—the one she hated so much. "Never be so dependent on something you'll do anything to keep it."

Callie made a face. It could have been written specifically for her—and the situation at Willow's End. Not that she agreed with it. She couldn't bear the idea of leaving her home, any more than she could bear the idea of some stranger living here, changing things. She thrust the thought from her mind. It wouldn't happen. She wouldn't let it. And rule or no rule, neither would Julian.

She skimmed further down his list and began to giggle. Surely he hadn't written this one—not on purpose, at any rate.

Julian stuck his head into the room, beads of water from his shower gleaming in his hair. "What's so funny? My rules aren't supposed to be funny, you know."

Brutus slinked over to one corner and Callie wiped the grin off her face. "It's rule number seven."

"Yeah? So? 'Your workplace should be like your mind,' he quoted, 'Channeled, Harmonious, Adaptable, Organized and Serious.' What's your problem?"

"Oh, I agree with it," she hastened to say. Her gaze snagged on a droplet of water inching down the tanned hollow of his throat to his breastbone. She licked her lips. "I...I mean, it's not what you're saying. It's..."

"Out with it, sweetheart. What's wrong with it?"

"It's chaos."

Julian walked into the room, yanking a shirt over his head. Callie fell back a pace, trying in vain to control her breathing. The man did incredible things to T-shirts. Or they did incredible things to him. Bright red cotton lovingly outlined every ripple and curve of his chest. Her glance dropped lower. His cutoffs weren't bad either, she decided, admiring the unending length of muscled leg the shorts bared to her view.

"You think it's chaotic?" he repeated, looking none too pleased.

"What?" She yanked her gaze back to his face.

He scowled. "That rule's the least chaotic one I've got. In fact, none of my rules are chaotic. Not a single one."

Callie struggled to return her attention to the conversation. "Not chaotic." Maybe she shouldn't have brought this up. "It spells chaos. You know, an acronym. All those words make an acronym that spells chaos."

He snatched his list of rules and studied them. "Damn. You're right." He looked at her, his brown eyes filled with a wry gleam. "You would notice something like that."

She lowered her eyes modestly. "I always do."

"You know, you continue to amaze me." He tossed the list onto his desk.

"It's not so bad," Callie comforted him. "All you need to do is change the order of your wording to spell something else. Like... like... 'Hocas' wouldn't work." She brightened. "How about 'casho'? You should like the sound of that."

His expression spoke volumes, but all he said was, "Thanks for the suggestion. And I thought the attic would prove the highlight of my day. Shows how wrong you can be."

"Was it that bad?" she sympathized.

"Have you been up there recently? It has cobwebs the size of Cincinnati."

"I warned you about that." She glanced across the room, her critical gaze coming to rest on the antique highboy pushed against one wall. The attic wasn't the only thing with cobwebs. It was all too apparent this room hadn't been cleaned in weeks. She'd have to do something about that. Soon.

"And those cobwebs had spiders to match. Big hairy ones..."

She continued to stare at the walnut chest of drawers. "Julian, what's Aunt Maudie's rose vase doing over there?"

"What?"

She pointed at the large squat vase resting on the top of the highboy. "Her rose vase. She always kept it in the library. What's it doing up here?"

Brutus whined mournfully, then crossed over to her and grabbed a piece of her shirt in his mouth. He pulled, tugging her toward the door to the hallway.

Callie pushed him away. "Stop it, Brutus. I don't want to go out. I want to see that vase." He released her shirt and shook his head. She looked down at him. His actions arousing her suspicions. "It's in there, isn't it? Something to do with Maudie's will?"

He shook his head again. "I don't believe you," she told him and started toward the highboy. Brutus barked sharply. When that failed to stop her, he whirled and ran from the room. Callie didn't bother to question his odd behavior. All her attention was focused on the vase.

"You think it's in there?" Julian asked, following her. "Why?"

"Because that particular vase doesn't belong in here. It belongs in the library. Maudie always kept it there and always, *always* kept it filled with flowers. Mostly roses, which is how it got its name." She waited for the significance of that fact to sink in. "Remember her other note? The one we found in the library? The one requesting we plant flowers in her memory?"

Julian began to grin. He reached up and lifted down the piece of porcelain and peered into its cavernous depths. With a cry of triumph, he reached inside and pulled out a pink rose-scented envelope. "Clever, Callie. Very clever. A bit of a stretch, but well done, nonetheless."

Her heart pounding wildly, Callie slit the envelope open and pulled out the single sheet of paper. Aloud she read:

"Dear Callie and Julian,
Very, very good, my dears. You've found my final note. Now you must find my will. Not that I'm going to make it easy for you. As I've always said, it's not worth getting if it's gotten too easily."

"When did she say that?" Julian demanded. "I never heard her say any such thing. 'Simple is as simple does,' she'd say. Or, 'If you can't do it right, don't bother doing it at all.' Not once did she ever say any of that 'not worth getting' business. Not once."

"I think I heard her say it," Callie admitted. At Julian's black frown, she hastened to add, "But only once, I'm sure." She glanced back at the note. "Why don't I just finish this?

"...if it's gotten too easily. (Though if Julian, with his love for classical literature doesn't figure out this clue, I'll be very disappointed.)"

"What the devil is she talking about now?" Julian complained. "I hate classical literature."

"You're interrupting again. Would you please be still and let me finish?" Callie rattled the paper and kept reading:

"...I'll be very disappointed.) Ready? Here's the clue: 'You, too?' Get it? Of course you did, smart boy. I knew you loved the classics."

"I hate the classics! Stop saying I loved them."
"Julian, hush.

"I love you both. Maudie."

"That's it? That's all she wrote?"

"P.S. Are you two friends again? Actually I'm hoping by now you're much more than friends. Has my plan worked?"

Julian thrust a hand through his hair, his impatience visible in every line of his body. "We've been put through all this because Maudie wanted to play matchmaker?'' He scowled, admitting grudgingly, ''I guess you can't argue with success.''

''Sweet of her, isn't it? There's another postscript:

P.P.S. Don't let Jonathan get his hands on Willow's End. He'll only sell it for one of his mad adventures.''

''Of course Jonathan will sell it,'' Julian groaned. ''Darn it, Maudie. If you didn't want that to happen, why didn't you just tell us where the damn will is, instead of playing Cupid?''

''Julian, you're being very irreverent. Besides, you're talking like she can actually hear you. Do you realize how strange that is?''

''That from a woman who talks to beagles and tulips?''

''Saint Bernards and daffodils.''

''Case in point. You realize we'll have to burn this note. It's the only way. If my father ever reads it, he'll have Maudie declared insane. And he'll get away with it, too. Because no one in their right mind would believe that the woman who wrote this bunch of nonsense could possibly be of sound mind and body.''

''I resent that! That's my Aunt Maudie you're talking about.''

''*My* Aunt Maudie. And resent away, sweetheart. It won't change the facts.'' He snapped his fingers. ''I've got it. Come on.'' He practically ran from the room.

Callie raced after him. ''You know what it means? You've figured it out?'' She followed him into the library, watching in dismay as, in a very un-Julian-like manner, he thrust through the piles of books decorating the floor. ''What are you looking for?''

"There's a book of quotes in here somewhere... Aha!" He snatched up a thick volume. "You, too... you, too... If it's a quote from something classical, it should be listed here." He scanned the table of contents, then flipped back to the index. Meticulously, he went through all the listings beginning with *you.* "Nothing." With a snort of disgust, he snapped the book closed and tossed it down.

"She had to get the idea you like classical literature from somewhere. Where?"

"Thin air?"

"Julian, be serious."

"I am. I haven't the vaguest notion where she got *any* of her ideas, least of all this one."

"She must have seen you reading Hemingway or Thoreau or Shakespeare or something. Think! You had to have done something to give her that impression."

Brutus stuck his head around the corner and peeked in at them. Julian stared at the door. His eyes narrowed. "No. It couldn't be."

"What? What is it?"

"It's too ridiculous. Not even Aunt Maudie... You, too? Could she have meant... And you? *Et tu?*" He took a step toward the door, his eyes fixed on Brutus, his hands closing into fists. "You mangy mutt. You had it all the time, didn't you? And dear Aunt Maudie. What a memory. She remembered I played Julius Caesar in my senior year of high school."

He began to quote. "'Doth not Brutus bootless kneel? Et tu, Brute?—then fall, Caesar!' Shakespeare. Act Three, Scene One. I *hated* that play."

He advanced on the Saint Bernard, his grin not a pleasant sight. "Here, doggy. Let's see what's in that old brandy cask."

Brutus backed away as fast as his bulk would allow. Then, with a yelp of terror, he took off running, with Julian hot on his tail.

"Julian, wait! You've scared him," Callie cried. She hurried after them, wincing at the loud crashing noises coming from the kitchen. Her poor pots and pans. She'd left them all over the floor. She wondered if any would survive. By the time she got there, man and dog were gone and the back door stood wide open. Her pots and pans lay scattered from one end of the room to the other.

Ignoring the mess, she stepped outside into the cool night air. The sun had set long ago, but there was a surprising amount of light. The moon was full and bright, the sky dusted with more stars than she could count in a lifetime. She looked down to the lake, expecting to see Brutus and Julian locked in mortal combat. The water, a perfect reflection of the sky above, lapped peacefully against the sandy shore.

Where were they? She studied the lawn, noticing the flattened spots in the long grass where feet had crushed a pathway. With a determined stride, she followed it around to the front of the house—and found her quarry on the front porch.

"Brutus, get off Julian," she ordered in exasperation. "That's no way to act."

Her words had absolutely no effect. Brutus continued to perch on Julian's back, oblivious to the muffled threats emanating from the man beneath him.

Callie climbed the porch steps. "Julian's only trying to get the will out of your brandy cask. It is in there, isn't it?" Brutus gave what she assumed was a woof of agreement. "Then what's the problem?"

"Would you stop arguing with the miserable mongrel and get him off me?"

"I'm trying," Callie snapped. "In case you hadn't noticed, he doesn't want to cooperate. Maybe if I found out why he's being so stubborn—"

"I can't believe this."

"—we might be able to reach a compromise." She put her hands on her hips. "I don't think he fully appreciates the ramifications of our situation."

"I don't think *you* fully appreciate the ramifications of *my* situation. I'm on the verge of being made a total cripple and you're talking like someone from *Sesame Street*. Don't compromise with him. Don't cooperate with him. Just get him the hell off my back!"

She glared at Julian. "Okay, fine. Be that way." She turned her fiercest look on Brutus. "You asked for this, so don't say you weren't warned. If you don't get off of Julian right this instant, you now and forever more will be nothing but a dog to me."

She folded her arms across her chest, waiting. Not that it took long. In two seconds flat, Brutus was sitting beside Julian instead of on top of him. "Give us the brandy cask." The dog backed away and Callie sighed.

"What's the problem now?" Julian asked, managing to sit up.

"He won't hand it over."

"Maybe because he doesn't have any hands! Try finding out what the problem is."

Callie grinned. "Really? You want me to reason with him? You're willing to do that all of a sudden?"

Julian ran a hand through his hair. "I'm willing to do anything that will get us that cask. Talk to him, jump him, paint him blue with purple polka dots. Just get it."

She shook her head in disappointment. "You refuse to understand, don't you? Even knowing about Brutus, you still treat him as if he's a dog."

"He *is* a dog!"

Callie ignored him. "If Brutus doesn't want to give us the will, there's probably a very reasonable explanation." Brutus endorsed her statement by rushing to Callie's side and rubbing up against her. "See?"

Julian gritted his teeth. "Hey, given half the chance, I'd rub up against you, too. Think of the time we've lost searching for that blasted will. Time we could have spent... rubbing."

"Julian!" Callie protested in shocked tones, secretly thrilled to her toenails. "Not in front of Brutus."

"Let him get someone of his own," he griped. "Until then, get that will. Explain it to the mutt, if you're so sure he understands everything. Tell him what will happen if we don't get that will."

Comprehension dawned in Callie's eyes and she snapped her fingers. "That's it. Brutus was never around when we discussed it before." She knelt down and gathered Brutus's huge face in her hands. "Listen to me, sweetheart. I'm sure you have a very good reason for keeping that will from us, but if we don't get it, Jonathan inherits everything." She paused, before adding significantly, "And that includes you."

Brutus let out an ear-splitting howl of anguish. Then he flopped over onto his back in the best "dead dog" imitation Callie had ever seen. She glanced at Julian who was struggling to his feet.

"I told you," she said. "He didn't know your father would inherit Willow's End or he'd have given the will to us in the first place. None of this would have happened if you'd talked to him, instead of treating him as if he were an animal or something." She walked over to Brutus, unstrapped the cask from around his neck and handed it to Julian. "Happy now?"

"No, I'm not happy now. I'm not even mildly contented."

He grabbed her around the waist and hauled her up against him, planting a warm lingering kiss on her lips. He started to release her, then apparently changed his mind, pulling her more fully into his arms. He cupped her face and kissed her with such loving passion it brought tears to her eyes.

"Now that," he whispered against her mouth, "goes a long way toward making up for things." He hesitated and gently tucked a strand of hair behind her ear. "Remember, sweetheart, no matter what it says, no matter who inherits, it's people that count." He started to add something, then shook his head. "Come on. Let's go inside and find out whether it's been worth the effort. We'll use my office."

Brutus made a mad dash ahead of them. When they arrived at the office, he sat waiting for them. Julian cleared his papers off the table and ceremoniously deposited the brandy cask there.

They both sat down and stared at it.

"Why don't you open it?" Callie suggested. "After all, you figured out Maudie's final clue."

"Which I wouldn't have done if you hadn't found her note," Julian pointed out.

"All right," she decided. "I'll open the cask and you read the will." She picked up the miniature barrel and looked for an opening. "Tell you what," she said, handing it to Julian. "You open it and I'll read the will."

He grinned and slipped his thumbnail into a nearly invisible slit, popping the two halves apart. Out fell a long narrow envelope marked "Last Will and Testament of Maude Margaret Hannigan."

"We found it," murmured Callie. "We actually found it." She shivered. "You read it. I don't think I can."

Brutus groaned and dropped his head onto her lap, his eyes huge and sad. Absently Callie rubbed his ears.

Julian opened the envelope and pulled out the typed pages, scanning them. "It's been signed and dated. Looks genuine enough. We'll have to have Peters look it over, but at least it's been witnessed and notarized."

"That's a relief. Do you think we should read it?" Brutus whined softly and Callie scratched his neck.

Julian shook his head, staring down at the papers in his hands. "Seems strange, doesn't it? I mean, we've spent so much time looking for this and yet, I'm hesitant to read it."

"Because this makes it final," Callie whispered. "She's dead and this confirms it."

With great deliberation, Julian turned to the first page. "Give me a minute to get to the pertinent information and then I'll read it to you."

There were four pages and it didn't take him long to get through them all. When he reached the end, he flipped to the front and read it again. Then he picked up the envelope and looked inside, taking out a single sheet of stationery. Quickly he read that.

Julian adjusted his glasses. "Well, green eyes, seems we've got a problem."

CHAPTER EIGHT

Rule #9:
Great lists are made,
not born.

BRUTUS LET OUT a mournful moan and Callie stiffened, her heart beginning a rapid tattoo. "A problem?" she questioned faintly. "With the will? No... Surely, Jonathan didn't...?"

Julian dropped the papers to the table and reached for her hand. "No. Not Jonathan. *We* inherit everything, Callie. You and I, jointly. Maudie left a letter of explanation." A small smile edged the corners of his mouth. "Seems she's determined to play matchmaker."

Callie stared at him in bewilderment. "So what's the problem?" She stumbled to a halt, embarrassment flooding through her. "Is it because she wants you and me to...? She hopes we'll...?"

He squeezed her hand, quick to reassure her. "I can't fault Maudie for hoping we'll get together. It's the only positive thing to come out of this whole mess." Her delight at his admission was short-lived. He released her fingers and stood up, rubbing a hand across his brow. "There's no money, Callie. Or damned little. And since we both inherit, nothing changes—our problems, unfortunately, remain. In fact they increase, because now we have to make a definite decision about Willow's End."

She fought to control her panic. "We can work it out. I know we can. I admit, planning things and saying no to volunteer work, and putting my foot down with Ted and the kids, aren't my strong points. But, don't you see? This is perfect. Those are *your* strong points. We'll work together and have it all—Brutus *and* Willow's End."

"Callie—"

Fear crept into her voice. "Now that you share custody of Brutus, you'll have to be nice to him. No more name calling or nasty threats." She leaned down and hugged the dog. "That's why you didn't want Julian to find the will, isn't it? But there's nothing left to fear." *Please let there be nothing left to fear!* "He understands about you now. Everything will be just like it was."

Julian interrupted. "No, it won't."

"I know, I know. Maudie's not here," she hastened to say, desperate to keep talking so that Julian wouldn't—couldn't. "And I realize your work is in Chicago, but..."

She ran out of words, too selfconscious to finish her sentence—at least until they'd made some sort of commitment. And so far that hadn't happened. Tears stung her eyes, tears she resolutely forced back. He cared about her. She didn't doubt that for a minute. She watched as he traced a fond hand across Maudie's antique highboy. He also cared about Willow's End. Suddenly she had to know the truth—had to know what he intended.

"What are we going to do about the house?" she asked abruptly. The words hung between them. Then Julian dropped his hand to his side. It was such a telling gesture. She knew then, knew beyond a shadow of a doubt how he felt, and a cold numbness stole over her. Silently she shook her head. "You want to sell, don't you," she whispered. "You still don't think I'm capable of coping."

"Callie—"

Fury ignited within her. "You can't! Not after what we've been through to find the will. Not after..." She met his eyes, defiance in every line of her body. "Not after what's happened between us."

He crossed to her side and grasped her shoulders. "What happened between us has nothing to do with it."

She fought free of his hold and jumped to her feet. "It has everything to do with it! The best things in your life are right here in this house, only you're too blind to realize it. Stop thinking with your head for a minute, and think with your heart."

"I am thinking with my heart. I don't want to sell Willow's End. It's my home, too! But I've got to consider what's best for you."

"Willow's End *is* best for me!"

He stepped closer to her, speaking in a low passionate voice. "This house is falling down around your ears. You haven't the money or the skill to complete the repairs. If you weren't so stubborn, you'd see this place is an impossible burden."

"It's not a burden!"

Julian ignored her interruption. "It isn't just the house. It's all the other problems, as well. How do you think I feel when I see people taking advantage of you, when you give away your last nickel to clean some stupid statue, when you wear yourself down doing favor after favor? I can't stand it, Callie. Nor will I stand idly by and allow it to happen. Not when I can do something to prevent it."

"Like taking away my home?" Her voice rose an octave. Brutus bounded up beside her, a soft husky growl rumbling in his throat. She placed a restraining hand on him and, forcing her voice back to a more normal pitch, continued, "I know, legally, you could force the sale. If you demanded your share of the inheritance, I don't doubt for a minute that some judge would order Willow's End to be sold and the profits split between us. Isn't that how it works?''

"Yes,'' he admitted.

"And you'd do that to me?''

Julian hesitated. "Callie, I don't want to hurt you—''

"Hurt me!'' She lifted her chin and glared at him. "If you felt anything for me at all, if you cared for me in the slightest, you wouldn't do it. You couldn't!''

"I wish I didn't have to,'' he said in a weary voice. "But I don't see any other way. Not if I want to live with myself afterward.'' He looked around, his expression almost bitter. "Sometimes I think this place means more to you than I do. When do we ever have time for ourselves? Willow's End is always in the way.''

His comment hit home. Willow's End did stand between them. It always would, unless they could reach an agreement—one they *both* could live with. She bit down on her lower lip, willing the tears from her eyes. This was neither the time nor the place to give in to such a childish display. Not when she needed every ounce of ruthless determination she possessed. Brutus gave her hand a supportive lick, which ironically, almost proved her undoing.

Callie forced herself to speak. "I can think of one way around it.''

"Which is?''

"You don't think I can handle things here on my own—that it's too much for me. If I prove to you that's not true, by following through on our former agreement, would you be willing to forgo selling the house?''

"Explain.''

She'd gotten his attention. Now she needed his consent. "We up the stakes on our bet. I say no to any and all favors for one week and you go without your watches and schedules. The winner determines the final disposition of Willow's End.''

"You must be joking."

Callie shook her head. She'd never been more serious in her life—nor more desperate. She had nothing to lose, and everything to gain. "My school testing and your work on the book don't count as part of the bet. If at the end of seven days neither of us has lost, I'll be considered the winner. After all, I'll have proved I can take care of myself."

What had started out as a small wager, a lighthearted joke between them, was rapidly turning into something else.

Julian took his time deciding. Finally he nodded. "I agree to the terms." He pulled off his glasses and stared at her, his eyes dark and remote. "What if you lose?"

Callie didn't hesitate an instant. "That's not a possibility," she said.

THE LIBRARY ECHOED with the battle cries of the two boys.

"Oh, yeah?" five-year-old Tommy screeched, his face beet-red with anger. "Well, mine has sixty-four different positions and that doesn't even count his robot form. Your stupid toy can only do thirty-eight."

"Liar! Liar! Mine does ten trillion hundred! And my dad can whop your dad to dust, no problem." David punctuated his comment by sticking out his tongue. "So there."

"Oh, yeah?"

"Yeah!"

Callie hurried into the room and pulled the two combatants apart before they came to blows. "David. Please remember that we keep our tongues in our mouths. And Tommy, we use our indoor voice when we're in the house. Surely you haven't forgotten that from kindergarten so soon?"

She glanced at their respective mothers, both of whom smiled benignly at the children, not in the least put out by the ruckus. Of course they weren't put out, Callie thought, tempted to knock a few heads together. It wasn't their house being destroyed.

She felt like finding a quiet hole, crawling in it and pulling the lid on after her. Instead she said, "If you could be patient a few more minutes, we'll have you tested and through as quickly as possible."

"Such a shame the school's being painted and it's out of commission for the next few weeks," commented David's mother with stoic disregard. "I hear they tried the library, but the air-conditioning broke down a few days ago. We wouldn't want poor Davey to suffer because of that. This testing is bad enough."

Callie bit her tongue.

"It's more convenient for Callie to do the testing in her own home," Tommy's mother added. "Suzanne Ashmore said so."

And because Suzanne said so, that was that. Callie almost made the comment out loud. Instead she sighed. How strange that she now resented many of the little things she'd done so willingly before.

It was all Julian's fault, darn him. If he hadn't planted the seeds of discontent, she'd never be thinking these horrible, petty, selfish thoughts. It wasn't like her.

This ridiculous bet had her rattled. Three days he'd managed to get through. Three days without a single slip. How was he doing it? She'd stopped all the clocks in the house and hidden the calendars. Not that it bothered Julian. Heavens, no! He'd managed just fine.

She, on the other hand, had been late for every one of her testing appointments. Not only that, but she now realized that winning the bet wouldn't be the snap she'd assumed. How could she ever have thought it would be easy? Callie groaned. Easy? Reasoning with a rhino would be easier than saying no to the multitude of favors she'd been asked over the past seventy-two hours. Nor was saying no all she had to contend with.

In the past six hours alone, she'd coped with fractious children and their equally fractious parents. She'd fought against an anger and frustration alien to her nature. And she'd begun to wonder if Julian hadn't been right in his assessment of her—or at least in part.

She'd begun to suspect that Callie Marcus was a pushover. The day was only half over and already she found herself exhausted, close to tears and very, very miserable.

Tommy's mother cleared her throat and looked pointedly at her watch.

Callie sighed again. Perhaps she could restart one clock. Just a little inconspicuous one that Julian wouldn't know about.

"I'm almost finished with Joannie Baker," Callie informed the mothers. "If you could keep everyone quiet for a few more minutes—"

"Hello? Hello?" Two more mothers came through the front door with what seemed like half-a-dozen four-year-olds in tow. "Is this where they're conducting the kindergarten testing? Suzanne Ashmore sent us over."

It took every ounce of Callie's self-control to keep from bursting into tears. It wasn't fair. Dear sweet Julian sat sunning by the lake with Donna and Cory, while she slaved away indoors testing obnoxious little—

She brought herself up short. Surely she hadn't been about to call these precious youngsters—she gulped—brats? She put a hand to her brow. Perhaps she'd caught a bug. That was it. She was ill. Very ill. Which explained her abnormal behavior. Well, thank goodness for that. She felt much better now.

"Everyone sit down," she ordered tersely. Sick people weren't expected to be sweet and cheerful. Sick people were permitted to be a bit grumpy. "Pretend this is a library and be *quiet.* I'll get to you when I can." With that she spun around and left the room. Though not soon enough.

"Well! If she thinks I'm going to expose my little Ashlee to such an unhealthy attitude..."

Callie didn't hear the rest. She closed the door behind her with more force than necessary. *One step at a time,* she told herself, taking a deep breath. *One rotten kid at a time.* And when she'd finished with the very last one, she'd never ever speak to Suzanne Ashmore again.

CALLIE AWOKE from her nap on the den couch, delighted to find herself wrapped in Julian's arms. How he'd managed to maneuver in beside her, she had no idea. Not that she intended to complain. Discovering her body molded to his, his mouth inches from her own, their hearts beating in tandem, gave her an indescribable surge of pleasure. What had started out as a truly rotten day now took a decided turn for the better. She settled deeper into his embrace, needing the loving comfort he offered.

"I wish we could always wake up like this," she murmured, her lips touching his throat. Then she blushed, realizing how suggestive her comment had sounded.

His chuckle rumbled against her lips. "I'd like to wake up every morning with you, too."

"I...we..." She cleared her throat. "There's a lot to settle before we take things any further. Isn't there?"

He inhaled deeply, and she nearly choked on her words. She could feel each hard firm muscle, sinew and tendon in his chest. She longed to grab back her words and eat every syllable.

"I suppose you're right," he muttered.

"We wouldn't want to rush into anything." She gazed up at him hopefully. "Would we?"

"No."

Then why did his arms tighten around her, as though he dreaded letting her go? And why did she cling to him, as though afraid they'd be snatched apart at any minute? She could feel him tense and knew he was on the verge of pulling away. She didn't want their embrace to end. Not yet. She squeezed her eyes closed, willing it to continue for a few minutes more.

Julian groaned. "I'm saying one thing, but what I feel is far different. If I don't let you go soon, I might do something we'll both regret later."

She buried her face in his shoulder, sliding her hands along the back of his neck. "Would that be so bad?"

"Maybe not. But I'd rather not take the chance." He rested his chin on top of her head. "I want you, Callie. I want to steal you away from here. I want to take you where there aren't any home-repair projects, or screaming kids, or crazy wills or screwy electrical repairmen. I think the next time someone asks you to do a favor, I'll toss you over my shoulder and carry you so far from here we'll never find our way back."

Her breath caught and she eased out of his arms. "You mean abandon Willow's End? I couldn't do that."

He swore softly yet virulently. "When will I ever learn? This house always comes first with you, doesn't it?" He stared up at the ceiling, a muscle working in his jaw. "So many times I've wondered who you love the most—me or this house. I don't dare ask you to choose between us, because I know I'd lose."

Callie started in dismay. "No, Julian, you've got it all wrong. You don't understand."

"You're right." He took a deep calming breath, speaking with a gentleness and compassion she'd never heard him use before. "So explain it to me. Why are you dead set against selling Willow's End?" He gave her waist a light squeeze to stem her hasty retort. "Take a minute and think about it. You know things can never be as they were when Maudie was alive. The house holds a lot of wonderful memories, true, but it's just a house. This could be your chance for a new start. Why don't you want to take it?''

She'd been waiting for this question, but that didn't make it any easier to answer. Still, she owed Julian a truthful response. She settled her head more comfortably against his shoulder.

''I've never told anyone else this.'' She gave it a moment's thought and amended, ''Except Brutus. Maudie knew how I felt without my having to put anything into words. You see—'' she offered the simple explanation ''— I love Willow's End. Truly love it. The years I've spent here have been the happiest of my life. Have you any idea what it was like for me before I moved to Willow?''

He inclined his head. ''Knowing Helene, I can guess.''

Her fingers curled against his chest and she laughed without humor. ''Yes, you can guess. But you'd never fully appreciate it, unless you lived it. I don't even remember my real father. He died when I was a baby. Until I came here, the longest I ever stayed any place was thirteen months. We were always on the move. And Mother changed husbands with about as much frequency as residences. Your father was my fourth 'daddy.' ''

It took her a minute to continue. She didn't often think about those years; they'd been unpleasant and unhappy. She'd worked hard to put them behind her and, thanks to Maudie, she'd done so. She shivered within the comfort of his arms.

''When we moved here, I thought I was in some sort of magical fairy tale.'' She closed her eyes, savoring the memory. ''I knew I'd found my true niche in the world. Maudie understood. When Mother decided she'd had her fill of rusticating among the farmers—her expression, not mine—Maudie was the one who saw to it that I remained behind.''

Julian regarded her thoughtfully. ''I don't remember any of this. It must have been the year I left for graduate school. How did Maudie manage to pull it off?''

''It wasn't difficult. Staying on in Willow was supposed to be a temporary thing until Mother could get relocated.'' Callie shrugged, shifting to a more comfortable position. ''After a while she began to realize how much freer her life was without a sixteen-year-old daughter around. When Maudie insisted I stay, Mother didn't put up much of a fight. I guess she was glad for the excuse to leave me behind.''

The word Julian used brought color to her cheeks, but Callie gazed at him unwaveringly. ''Maybe now you'll understand why Willow's End means so much to me, why I don't want to sell it. When you go as long as I did without a home, you'll do whatever it takes to keep it and care for it.'' Her words had been revealing, and Callie looked away, uncomfortable with betraying so much.

Julian spoke in a low intense tone. ''Call off the bet, Callie. Making it was a mistake.'' He gripped her shoulders, speaking rapidly. ''Forget about Willow's End. Move to Chicago and start a new life with me.''

She covered his lips with her fingers. ''No, Julian. This would always hang over us. It needs to be resolved before we can make those sorts of decisions. You haven't changed your mind about my ability to cope with running this place, have you?''

He released her and leaned his head back against the couch cushions. ''No, I haven't.''

''I thought not.'' She gave him a tremulous smile. ''Which is why I won't end the bet. I think it's done me more good than you may realize. I'm not just proving something to you anymore. I now have something to prove to myself."

He sighed. "Believe it or not, I want you to win. If the disposition of Willow's End falls on me, I can't promise you'll like the results. You know that, don't you?"

This time she stopped his words with her mouth. "Don't say any more, Julian," she breathed against his lips. "Don't spoil what we have. Not yet. Tomorrow it might all fall down around our ears, but for now let's enjoy our time together."

She lowered her head to his chest, hearing the strong even beat of his heart. She felt safe and protected within the tight circle of his arms—more at home there than anywhere else, even Willow. If only it could be forever. She squeezed her eyes closed. If only...

ON THE MORNING of the fourth day of the bet, Callie decided she needed to get organized. "The first thing we do," she informed Brutus, "is come up with some great new excuses for why I can't help people. I can't seem to just tell them no." She took a sip of her coffee and set the mug back down on the kitchen table. "Frankly I'm not altogether certain the word no is even in my vocabulary."

Brutus gave a little snort, which she took as a signal of agreement. "Oh, well. We'll have to manage somehow. Julian can't hold out much longer. We can outlast him, no problem."

Her staunch loyal supporter and friend whimpered.

Despite his lack of faith, she found that fourth day surprisingly easy—for the simple reason that no one phoned her and no one came by. The fifth day proved to be more difficult—again for a simple reason. The phone rang.

Callie reached for the receiver and looked down to see Brutus practically sitting on her feet.

"I know, I know. I won't blow it." Brutus rolled his eyes and she scowled at him. "Don't look at me like that. I know what I'm doing." She picked up the phone with one hand and held her nose with the other. "We're sorry. You have reached a number that has been disconnected or is no longer in service—"

"Callie?"

"If you feel you have reached this recording in error, please check the number and try your call again." She hung up on Valerie's confused sputterings and smiled smugly at Brutus. "See? A few more days of that and we're home free."

"Not a chance."

Callie turned and her smug smile slipped a notch. "Oh. Hiya, Julian." She scuffed a toe on the white linoleum. "Been here long?"

He folded his arms across his chest. "Long enough to know you're not playing fair."

Her chin shot out an inch. "I don't remember anything being said about playing fair. I remember lots being said about favors, and saying no, and various what-ifs and therefores. But—" The phone rang again and they both turned to stare at it.

"Aren't you going to answer?" Julian asked on the third ring.

She shook her head. "I was sort of thinking I wouldn't."

Julian heaved a deep sigh. "I'm disappointed in you, Callie. You are not getting into the spirit of the thing."

"Tough."

"Answer it!"

Callie snatched up the receiver. "What do you want?" she barked into the phone.

"Callie? Is that you? What on earth is going on?"

"I can't do it."

There was a long pause and then Valerie said in a confused voice, "Can't do what?"

"Whatever it is you called me about. I can't do it. Call me next week. Goodbye." She slammed the phone down and faced Julian, her hands on her hips. "There. Are you satisfied now?"

He shook his head and chuckled. "Not exactly. Though it's a conversation that will live long in my memory. Next time try letting them ask you the favor before turning them down."

"You do it your way and I'll do it mine."

"And you'll be lynched before the week's out."

The phone rang and Callie groaned. She couldn't go through it again. It wasn't in her nature to be rude and surly. If she picked up the phone, she'd start apologizing all over the place and end up promising to do every favor in the book from now until next Christmas.

She'd be firm. She'd be firm and keep saying no. She snatched up the message pad beside the phone and wrote NO in big letters. She glared at Julian. "And stop laughing. This isn't funny." She picked up the phone again.

"Hello?" she inquired sweetly.

"Hello, Callie. Brad Anderson here. Could you get Julian for me? It's urgent."

She fluttered her eyelashes at Julian. The fink. "Gee, I'm sorry, Brad. If I called Julian to the phone that would be doing you a favor. It would be doing him a favor. That's two favors. And I'm not allowed to do *any* favors." Before Julian could get to her, she banged the phone down and took off at a run.

THE SIXTH DAY was nearly her undoing. Word, she decided, had gotten around. Probably thanks to Julian. She wouldn't put it past him to broadcast the details of her bet to the entire town of Willow, just so he could sit back and watch the fun. She was oh, so tempted to take the phone off the hook. But she refused to do it. She would win their wager, and she'd win it fair and square—which meant not telling anyone why she needed to refuse all requests.

Or so she thought until Valerie called.

"Am I still your friend, or aren't I?" Valerie opened the conversation on a plaintive note.

Callie cleared her throat. "That depends. What do you want?"

"That's what I'm talking about. What is all this about what I want? Can't I just call you up for a simple chat?"

"Oh, you want to talk. Great," Callie sighed, sliding down in her chair. "I can do that. Talk."

"I mean what's so wrong about asking a friend for a little favor? Explain it to me. Have I been unreasonable? Have I presumed too much on our friendship? What's the deal?"

"Favor?" Callie sat up straight, alarm coursing through her. "Oh, please, don't use that word. It's really an unpleasant word and I know you don't want to say it quite that way. How about, you were wondering if I would like to...? Or did I remember how I'd been meaning to...? Something that doesn't use that f-word."

"I'd like to borrow your beach and water toys. The ones you always drag out for the little kids to play with at the lake. We're leaving at two o'clock sharp to visit my mother and I'd hoped you could bring them by. Now is that too much to ask?"

Callie struggled for that n-word she'd been trying to use all week. "Now?" was all she could come up with.

"Not now. Two o'clock."

She fought off the nearly overwhelming impulse to agree. After all, Willow's End meant more than a pile of toys. "I can't," she said instead, and smiled. It might not be a *no*, but it came darned close.

"Callie, I'm desperate. If it's a problem to drop them off, I can always swing by and pick them up. Will that do?" Valerie didn't wait for an answer. There was a cheery "Thanks. You're the best." And the line went dead.

CALLIE OPENED the closet door beneath the main staircase, arguing with Brutus as she searched. "Listen. This isn't really a favor. I pull this stuff out every summer. No big thing."

Brutus whined unhappily.

She ignored him and shoved the winter clothes to one side. Crouching down between the various boxes, boots, gloves and hats, she dug deeper into the closet.

"I'm not doing this because Valerie wants me to, but because I happened to be thinking about beach toys and realized we hadn't pulled ours out yet. That's not doing a favor. Not at all. And it certainly has nothing to do with the bet."

Brutus barked in protest.

She swiveled around and glared at him. "Okay. It's a sort-of favor. But if you don't tell him and I don't tell him, Julian will never know. And what Julian doesn't know won't hurt him." She turned back to the job at hand. Bending low, she spied a beat-up cardboard box. "Aha. Gotcha!"

Before she could grab hold of it, something whacked against her backside, sending her headlong into the depths of the closet.

Callie struggled to sit up, fighting off a winter coat that had somehow taken up residence on top of her head. Even without the coat, the pitch black made it impossible to see anything. She shoved a basketball to one side and started to crawl over the boxes and bags to the door.

"Hey!" she shouted. "What's going on? Who turned out the lights?" Her head hit the wall. "When I get out of here," she muttered, rubbing her forehead, "you dog, are one dead duck."

She felt along the wall until her hand hit the outline of the door. She searched for the knob and with a sigh of relief found it. She turned it and pushed. And pushed.

"Brutus couldn't have locked it," Callie told herself. "He's good, but he's not that good." She stood up and pounded on the door. "You're good," she yelled, "but you're not that good. You can't keep me in here forever." She frowned. "Can you?"

There was no light switch in the closet. Fumbling in the dark, she thrust a boot, a ball of yarn and a globe out of her way and then knelt down, her face against the floor. Everything was black, totally black. Experimentally she shoved her fingers into the tiny crack under the door. She hit fur.

"Why you...you..." She grabbed the doorknob and shook it as hard as she could. Moving two hundred pounds of stubborn dog was not going to be an easy task. "Get away from this door, you puffed-up poodle!" She stuck her ear to the wooden surface and heard a loud rumbling snore.

"I can't believe it," she muttered, sitting down crosslegged on the floor. "How can he possibly go to sleep?" She leaned against the wall, cradling the box of toys in her arms. Well, at least while she stayed locked in the closet, she wouldn't be tempted to do anyone a favor. She yawned and shut her eyes.

Sometime later the door opened and bright sunshine streamed in. Callie blinked and looked up at Julian. "Oh, hello," she greeted him. He stood silently for a long time, his gaze moving from her to the box of toys and back again.

"I don't think I'll ask," Julian said. "I think I'll just close the door and leave."

"Brutus locked me in here," she explained with a sleepy smile, holding up her hands to him. "Wasn't that mean of him?"

He reached down and tugged her to her feet, chuckling as she stumbled into his arms, scattering beach toys in her wake. "It was downright cruel, if you ask me," he said, and kissed her.

Nothing he could have done was guaranteed to wake her up more thoroughly. As she slid her arms around his neck and kissed him back, she could hear Julian groan deep in his throat.

"I want you," he informed her in a husky voice.

Reluctantly she pulled away, lifting a hand to trace the rough skin along his jaw. "I want you, too. So what do we do about it?"

"Slip back into the closet and close the door?"

She laughed, shaking her head. "Tempting, but not enough room to be workable." Suddenly she remembered Valerie. "What time is it? Is it past two?" She broke off. "Oh, that's right, you don't wear a watch anymore. How could I forget?"

His arms tightened around her. "I don't know," Julian murmured, his eyes gleaming with amusement. "How?"

"I guess I'm still half-asleep." She bent down and picked up the plastic bucket and shovel resting at their feet. "I was going to put these toys out when Brutus locked—" She stopped, realizing what she'd revealed. "That is, I... You see..."

Julian's lips twitched. "I see better than you might think, sweetheart. You don't suppose Brutus locked you in the closet to keep you from doing that very thing, do you?"

"Don't be ridiculous." Callie tossed the rest of the toys into the closet and shoved the door closed. "Really, Julian. Brutus is just a dog. The way you talk about him, you'd think he was human or something."

He choked on a laugh. "I notice you don't say that when the mutt is anywhere within hearing." He lifted her chin and she was forced to look at him. "I knew this bet wouldn't be easy for you. And I know how hard you're trying. You can do it, Callie. I know you can."

Her mouth turned down at the corners. "I'm not so sure."

"Think of it as a skill you need to learn. The art of saying no."

"But why?" she demanded in frustration. "Why do I have to say no all the time? I'd much rather say yes."

His lips brushed hers. "Shall I give you something to say yes to?"

"No," she retorted perversely. "Darn it, Julian. This isn't fair. You're expecting me to do something that goes against my basic nature."

"Not at all," he insisted. "I expect you to stand up for yourself when it's necessary. It's not that I want you to refuse all favors. I just want you to learn to be a little judicious about which favors you agree to do."

"Well, since I'm not allowed to do *any* favors, judicious or otherwise, I think I'll go call Valerie," she said with as much dignity as she could muster. "For a chat. Just for a chat. Certainly not about any beach toys, or any stupid bets."

But after calling and offering a lame excuse to an understanding Valerie, carefully omitting any mention of the bet, Callie thought about what he'd said. She thought about it a lot—all through the rest of the day—while Julian and the kids continued with the repairs on the house. She watched them work together, watched their growing rapport and their mutual respect. She watched the firm way he dealt with them, and their acceptance of it.

And she watched him. It was an easy enough task. In fact

it was an enjoyable task. She liked the way he moved with swift sure strides. She liked the way his brown eyes lit with pleasure when he laughed, or darkened to jet when he was annoyed. And she liked the way he'd take off his glasses to ponder a question, or thrust them high on his nose when he wanted to mentally distance himself from something or someone.

She loved him. She loved his laughter and his sense of humor—strange though it was. She even loved him for what he was attempting to do, though she didn't agree with his reasons.

What she didn't love were the doubts that plagued her. He'd said that he wouldn't make any promises about Willow's End should she lose the bet. And he certainly hadn't made any commitment to her, beyond the conditions of their wager.

Suddenly that wasn't enough. Willow's End wasn't enough. She wanted Julian, not a house. She wanted to be part of his life, to live with him and love him and have his children. Unfortunately he hadn't offered her that.

ON THE SEVENTH DAY, Callie realized she would win the bet. It gave her a sense of accomplishment, but it didn't give her the thrill she'd expected. Instead she realized that she'd rather have bargained for something quite different from Willow's End. If she could, she'd have bargained for Julian's love.

The phone rang and she picked it up without hesitation. "Hello? Yes, Mayor, what can I do for you?" She listened for a minute, then replied smoothly, "I appreciate you thinking of me for that committee, but I'm afraid I can't help you. Have you tried Suzanne Ashmore? She's always ready to lend a helping hand. Yes, maybe next time. Good talking to you, too."

Callie replaced the receiver and sighed. Well, if nothing else, she'd become quite adept at refusing to help. She just didn't know whether to consider that a positive achievement. The phone rang a second time and she reached for it, relieved that today ended the bet. This was tiresome. "Hello?"

"Callie? It's me," a muffled voice responded.

"Donna?" Callie frowned. "What's wrong? You sound strange."

The girl made a noise that sounded suspiciously like a sob. "It's Cory. Something's happened."

"What? What is it? Is he hurt?"

"No, he's not hurt. He's in trouble. I'm down at the police station. They...they've arrested him." This time there was no mistaking her tears. "Please, will you come?"

"Yes, of course." Callie spoke in a soothing voice. "Try to stay calm, Donna. I'm on my way. You're at Southside station?"

"Yes. Hurry, Callie. I'm frightened."

"I know you are. You did the right thing calling me. I'll be there in five minutes."

Callie hung up the phone and closed her eyes. She didn't question for a minute what she'd do. She'd go and help Cory. She didn't have any choice. Some things were more important than a bet or a house. Cory was more important. She grabbed her purse.

Regrets could come later.

CHAPTER NINE

Rule #100:
Rules were made to be broken.

CALLIE PULLED up outside the Southside police station and jumped out of her car. "What's happened?" she demanded of Donna, who came running up to her. "Where's Cory?"

"He's inside. The police think he's involved in another vandalism case. He didn't do it, Callie. He was at Willow's End at the time. But no one believes him." She glanced at the station house, a hint of fear in her blue eyes. "I think they've arrested him. If his parents find out he's in big trouble. Please, will you help?"

"Of course." Together they hurried into the station and up to the police officer at the front desk.

"Why, hello, Callie," Sergeant Collins said. "What's got you in such an uproar?"

"I've come about Cory Muldrew," she explained, giving Donna's hand a reassuring squeeze.

Fortunately it took no time at all to straighten out the situation. The officer in charge was only too happy to cooperate with Callie. They compared notes, and to their mutual relief, discovered Cory had been working at Willow's End at the time of the vandalism incident.

"I'm positive Cory couldn't have done it," she explained to Sergeant Collins. "If you need Julian to collaborate—"

"No, no. You take this young man on home with you and that'll be the end of it."

"Does that mean my parents don't have to know I was down here?" Cory asked. "If Dad finds out, he might want to sue for false arrest or something."

Callie muttered a rude word beneath her breath and grabbed Cory's shirt front. Before he could utter another sound, she yanked him out of the station and toward her car. Fifteen minutes later she was back at Willow's End—and exhausted.

She collapsed into a kitchen chair and dropped her head on her arms. So she'd lost the bet. So she'd lost Willow's End. She'd been true to her conscience and done the right thing. Julian would understand about right things and consciences. Sure he would. She sighed. And pigs around the world would sprout wings, rise up, and fly.

"Callie?"

She lifted her head and saw Julian standing by the kitchen door. He stepped toward her and she stared at him, unable to answer. Answering meant losing the bet and she wanted another few minutes with things the way they'd been. Just another minute to pretend that it would all work out. Another minute to savor the fantasy of Julian and Willow's End and Brutus together—and a part of her life.

He gave her a slow warm smile. "I looked for you a while ago. I thought you might like a swim. I'm afraid it's too late now." He indicated the suit he wore. "There's an emergency connected with work and I have to see a customer in Peoria."

His dark hair, still damp from a shower, clung to his skull in dark attractive waves. She stared at him. She couldn't help it. He was so precious to her, so important to her happiness and well-being—and so out of reach. Tears pricked her eyes. In a way, this was a goodbye. When he returned from his business call, things would never be the same between them.

"Are you all right?" he asked, his concerned gaze sweeping over her.

Callie almost smiled. "Sure." She was always "all right" whenever he was around. He seemed to have a magical ability to make things "all right" with her world.

He hesitated, apparently unwilling to leave. "Where did you go?"

"Out." She took a deep breath. She should tell him now and get it over with. Waiting wouldn't make the end result any easier to bear. "Julian..."

"Are you sure you're all right?" He approached the table and tossed his coat and briefcase onto a chair. "You're so...so quiet."

She stared at him, unable to say a word. His eyes were warm and loving, his expression open and relaxed. In a minute that would all change. *Tell him!* the words rang in her head. *Tell him now, before it's too late.*

"Oh. By the way, congratulations." He grinned at her look of confusion. "Come here. I have something for you."

She stood up. "Julian," she said in a rush. "I need to tell you—"

"Tell me later. This is more important."

He dropped his hands onto her shoulders and pulled her close. Callie breathed deeply, inhaling the scent of him. It was enough to make her dizzy. She slid her arms around his waist and leaned into his embrace, resting her head against the solid warmth of his chest. It felt so good to be held by him. Everything else paled to insignificance beside that fact.

"Congratulations, green eyes," he murmured, his lips caressing hers. "You did it. As of five minutes ago, you won the bet. I'll be honest, I had my doubts, but you pulled it off. I couldn't be happier."

Callie squeezed her eyes shut. It was sheer agony to listen to him, to feel his touch, knowing she didn't deserve any of it. She had to tell him the truth, even though she didn't think she could stand to watch the pride and pleasure die from his expression when he heard it. Once he learned what she'd done, he'd be forced to sell Willow's End. He'd have no choice.

Gently she disengaged herself from his arms. "Julian, there's something I have to tell you." She forced herself to meet his eyes. "I didn't win the bet. Donna called a little while ago. She and Cory needed my help. I couldn't refuse them."

Already she could sense his coolness. He didn't say anything, but behind his calm remote exterior, she knew his brain was working at a furious pace.

"We'll have to discuss this later," he said quietly. "There isn't time now. I'm sorry. If it weren't for this situation at work... We'll talk the minute I get back."

"Is there any point?" she whispered.

He cupped her face in her hands. "There's every point— if for no other reason than this..."

He leaned down and kissed her. His lips were hard and firm and made promises she wanted to believe. Callie clung to him. Her hands slid over his crisp cotton shirt and gripped his shoulders. Silently she pleaded with him, begging with urgent lips and arms for his understanding... for his love.

"Julian..." she whispered against his mouth.

He ran a hand through her hair, tugging it gently. "Be patient, Callie. We'll work it out. Trust me." And with that he picked up his briefcase and coat, and left.

Trust him, Julian had said. And she did. With her life. But not with Willow's End. He'd made no bones about his intentions—he wanted to sell. And thanks to her, now he could.

What she really needed right now, Callie decided, was either a good long cry or a hot cup of tea. More than anything, she wanted to cry. She settled for the tea. Crossing to the stove, she put on the kettle. The soft blue gas flame blurred before her eyes and she blinked hard, willing herself not to give in to tears.

Brutus trudged into the room and flopped down on the floor, his head turned away from her. "I know," she told him. "I blew it. I let everyone down. Rub it in, why don't you."

He let out a great gusty sigh.

"Guess I know where I stand with you," she muttered.

Yes, she knew where she stood. Absolutely nowhere. The tears became harder to blink away. How could helping Cory be so wrong? It wasn't. But that was beside the point. She'd wagered and lost.

If nothing else, that stupid bet had clarified things for her. It was her nature to give, just as it had been Maudie's. They shared that characteristic. Both of them were ready, willing and as happy as a pair of lovebirds to lend a helping hand. Callie scrubbed at cheeks that were unaccountably wet. If Julian didn't appreciate and understand that, then he didn't really love her.

"All right! Would someone mind telling me what's going on around here? I mean, enough is enough." Valerie shoved open the back door and walked in, her face set in determined lines.

Callie took one look at her friend and burst into tears.

Valerie exclaimed in consternation, "I knew it. I knew it! All those weird phone calls, those pathetic excuses you've been handing out to everyone. The whole of Willow's going on about how you've changed. They've decided Julian's a bad influence and should be run out of town. I said I'd talk to you first." She whirled on Brutus. "You! Beat it. I won't have any gloomy faces around here making things worse.

Besides, this is girl talk. And despite that operation you had, I still consider you mostly male."

With a huff, Brutus heaved himself to his feet and stalked from the room.

Valerie grasped Callie by the shoulders and led her to the kitchen table. "Sit. I'll fix the tea. Although by the look of you, a good stiff scotch would do more good." She hurried to the stove and poured boiling water over the tea bags. Then she placed the two steaming mugs on the table and sat down across from Callie.

"Now, spill it. What's going on around here?"

It seemed to take forever to get the entire story told, but eventually Callie ran out of words.

Valerie sipped her tea thoughtfully. "You want my honest opinion?"

Callie smiled weakly. "Can I handle it?"

"Probably not. But I'll tell you, anyway. Julian's right. People do take advantage of you. I take advantage of you." She waved aside Callie's cry of protest. "Oh, not deliberately. It's just that you're always so willing to help out. After a while people take your assistance for granted. Need someone to chair a committee? Ask Callie. Need a dozen cupcakes for the school social? Callie will do it. Need a baby-sitter for Tom, Dick or Danny? Callie loves kids."

"You make me sound like a pushover," she protested.

"Hey, if the goose honks when you squeeze it..." Valerie shrugged.

"If the goose..." Callie's eyebrows drew together. "That doesn't make a bit of sense."

"It doesn't have to," her friend retorted. "If it makes you stop and think, that's all that matters."

"Okay, okay. I'm thinking. And I've learned my lesson." Callie sighed. "What good does that do? I've still lost Willow's End."

"Did Julian say that?"

"He said he wanted to sell the house."

"*Wanted* to. That's a bit different than *going* to. Callie, he obviously cares a lot about you. Do you think for one minute that he *wants* to take Willow's End away from you? It sounds to me like he's been doing everything within his power to insure you win the bet."

Callie shook her head. "If he wanted me to win, why didn't he just agree to keep Willow's End in the first place?"

Valerie rolled her eyes. "Because he would have spent most of his time in Chicago worrying about what sort of disasters you were engineering down here. Think, girl! Do you realize how much he's risking by making this bet?"

"*He's* risking? I'm the one who'll lose Willow's End."

"He loses Willow's End, too," Valerie pointed out very softly and very distinctly. "Julian never said he didn't want the house. In fact, he hasn't considered himself in any of this. He said he wanted to sell because he was concerned about *your* welfare. He's thinking about what's best for you. And he cares enough to risk this new relationship of yours."

"I... I never thought of that," Callie stammered. "But what do we do now? I blew it. I mean, I didn't blow it. I had to help Cory. But I've lost the bet."

"I guess you decide what's more important to you. Willow's End or Julian."

Julian. The answer leapt unbidden to her mind. With regret she pushed her memories of Willow's End to one side. He'd been right. It wasn't the house that was important, but the people in it. And he was the most important person of all. "Thanks," she said with a wide smile. "I can't tell you how much easier that makes everything."

Valerie groaned in frustration. "Well, don't leave me in the dark. Which is it? Julian or Willow's End?"

Callie glared at her. "And you call yourself my best friend. You should know which I'll choose without asking."

Valerie grinned. "I do. But I still want to see that mushy look you get when you say his name."

LATER THAT AFTERNOON, the front doorbell rang. Thinking it might be Julian, Callie ran to let him in, Brutus at her heels. She realized her error the second she pulled open the door. Julian wouldn't have rung the bell; he'd have walked right in.

A tall good-looking man greeted her, sticking out his hand. "Hi," he said. "Brad Anderson."

"Of course," Callie said, shaking hands. "How are you, Brad? Would you like to come in?" Brutus growled low in his throat and Callie stared down at him in amazement. What had set him off? she wondered.

"I'd love to," Brad agreed with alacrity, though he hesitated to follow up on her offer. "Your dog won't bite, will he?"

"I'm not sure," Callie admitted honestly.

Julian's partner laughed, as though she'd made a joke, and Callie didn't quite have the nerve to tell him that she'd been dead serious. He stepped inside. To her relief, Brutus refrained from eating him then and there.

"Nice to see you again," Brad said, and smiled, his eyes revealing admiration. Though what he saw to admire, Callie wasn't quite sure. Between the tears she'd shed in the kitchen and her session with Valerie, she must look a mess.

She studied him uncertainly. "Julian isn't here. He had a business meeting in Peoria."

"I know. I just came from there. I stopped by to pick up some papers I need to take to our Chicago office." Brad patted his coat pockets and pulled out an envelope. "Julian said to give this to you."

Not caring what common courtesy demanded, Callie ripped it open and swiftly scanned the message. "Callie, give Brad whatever he wants. I'm sorry about the bet, we'll settle this business when I return." He'd signed the note with his initial, the single letter written in a strong slashing stroke.

Carefully she folded the paper in half and struggled to pin a smile on her face. It shouldn't come as any surprise. She'd known Willow's End was lost the minute she'd gone to help Cory. This only confirmed it. It hurt. She couldn't deny that. But it didn't come close to the hurt she'd feel if she lost Julian. Nothing was more important than their love—not even Willow's End.

"Listen," Brad said, "I don't want to rush you, but I need to get those papers." He looked around eagerly. "Though I also hoped you'd be willing to show me the house."

Callie stared at him in bewilderment. "You mean like a tour or something?" At his nod, she guessed, "Oh, you must want to see the changes Julian's made."

Brad shrugged. "If you think I should. I'm really more interested in the future potential of the place. Anything Julian's changed that I don't like, I can always change back."

Callie tilted her head to one side. He *looked* intelligent enough and his words were fairly straightforward. So why didn't she understand a thing he said? It must be because her brain was sluggish right now, she decided. Too many emotions had caused a short circuit or temporary brain damage. Something.

She recalled Julian's instructions. They'd been quite specific. Considering their present situation, she'd probably be wise to follow them. "Where would you like to start?"

"You don't mind? Somehow I thought you would."

"Julian said to give you what you wanted." She summoned a grin. "Do you want the grand tour or just the highlights?"

"The grand tour."

Callie took him to the dining room first, surprised that Brutus chose to tag along. She pointed out the improvements they'd made, not bothering to make a secret of her pride in their work. Repairing the coved ceilings had been particularly tricky.

"This is pretty good." He pointed to the door across the room. "Where does that go?"

"To the kitchen."

He frowned. "I suppose that won't be a problem." He winked at her. "Though knowing my wife, she'll probably want to knock down the wall and open up the two rooms."

Callie stared at him as though he'd gone insane. "So tell her no."

He burst out laughing and Callie began to wonder if she was the one who'd gone insane. "You haven't lost your sense of humor, I see," he declared. "That's good. Let's check out the kitchen." He went ahead, Callie and Brutus trailing in his wake. "Marie's going to have a fit when she sees this." He clicked his tongue in dismay.

"Your wife again?" Callie wanted to know. "And why is she going to have a fit over my kitchen? Er, Julian's kitchen?"

"Because she's heavy into chrome and modules. All this oak will send her right around the bend."

Well, of all the nerve! Callie put her hands on her hips. Enough was enough. She'd been willing to do the man a favor, but that didn't mean she had to put up with his insults. "Let me tell you what your Marie can—"

Brad crossed to the back door and looked outside. "And there's the lake. Lord, I love that lake. We used to spend our entire summer down there. Remember?"

"Vividly," Callie muttered.

"It does go with the house, doesn't it? No one else shares title to it?"

"No. Now listen—"

"Fantastic. Come on. Let's check out the other rooms."

Brutus snarled at Brad's retreating back. "You and me both," Callie said to him. "And Julian had the nerve to complain about Maudie. Maudie could have taken lessons from this guy." She shook her head. "Funny. I don't remember his being this strange."

She and Brutus found Brad in the library. "Would you mind holding this?" he asked, handing her one end of a measuring tape. "Now stand over by those windows while I see how much space we've got in here."

"Would you mind telling me—"

"Darn. Well, that's that, then. Those bookcases will have to come out. Marie's sauna won't fit otherwise."

"What? *What* sauna?" Forget the sauna, she told herself. He'd just said he was going to pull out Maudie's pride and joy—the bookcases. She let go of her end of the measuring tape, not one bit sorry when it whizzed across the room and snapped against his fingers. "Let me tell you something, here and now. You're not laying a hand on these bookcases. They're solid mahogany and over a hundred years old!"

"That old? Then they definitely come out. They've lived long past their usefulness, wouldn't you say?"

"No, I would not say. What do you mean coming in here and measuring this and threatening to knock down that? You don't own the place, you know."

"Not yet, maybe. But I will soon enough."

Callie felt like she'd just taken a shot to the jaw. She stared at him in shock, every bit of color draining from her face. "No," she whispered in disbelief. "That's impossible."

Brad groaned. "You didn't know? No wonder you were taking it so well."

"Julian—" Her voice broke and it took every ounce of determination to finish her question. "Julian is selling Willow's End to *you?*"

"He promised me right of first refusal."

"When? How ... ?"

"On the phone." Brad shrugged. "Just today I heard that he's got the controlling interest in Willow's End. And since he does ..."

And since she'd lost the bet ... Callie struggled to take it all in. Julian was really going through with it. He was going to sell her home. She shook her head. It seemed like a bad dream. He'd asked her to be patient. He'd kissed her and said to trust him. Surely he wouldn't sell without warning her, not when he'd promised to discuss it first? Her chin quivered and she reached blindly for Brutus. Seemed discussion time was over.

"You look like you could use some fresh air. Why don't we go outside?" Brad suggested. He took her by the arm and practically propelled her to the front door and out into the bright sunshine. He stopped beside the rose bed she and Julian had started for Maudie.

Callie took a deep breath, forcing herself to face facts. Julian intended to sell her home. She'd already accepted that, resigning herself to losing Willow's End. But what she refused to accept was his selling her home to Brad Anderson. Nor would she stand by and listen to how Brad and his wife intended to rip it apart, room by room. First the dining room. Demolished. Then the kitchen. Gutted. And then Maudie's library. Gone. All of it destroyed to make way for—she closed her eyes—an enlarged eating area, a modular kitchen and a sauna.

She reached out and touched a plump red rose with a gentle finger, fighting back tears. How could she bear it?

"Hey, Callie," a voice hailed her from the driveway. "What's happening?"

She turned, not certain whether the sight of Cory made the situation better or worse. Worse, if she gave in to her urge to cry.

"Callie?" Cory's brows drew together in concern. "What's wrong?" He glanced at Brad, his eyes mirroring his suspicion. "This guy buggin' you? Want me to punch him in the nose? After today, I owe you one."

Brad took a step away from Cory, clearly searching for an innocuous topic of conversation. "What pretty roses," he commented in an attempt to pour oil on troubled waters. "Too bad we're allergic to them." He sneezed as though to prove his point, then tossed a match on those oily waters. "Perhaps Marie could put in lilies instead."

"Lilies!" Callie's urge to cry dissipated beneath her fury. "Maudie hates lilies!"

There was a bone-chilling howl followed by a loud ferocious bark, and then Brad vanished beneath a blur of brown-and-white.

"Help!" came his muffled shriek.

"Get him, Brutus!" Cory hollered in encouragement. "'Cause if you don't, I will." He glanced at Callie. "You never did mention—what are we getting this guy for?"

Before Callie could respond, a car peeled into the driveway and Julian leapt out and came charging up the walkway. He jumped into the middle of the fracas, disappearing into the pile of fur, skin and suit. To her utter amazement he reemerged, Brad in one hand, Brutus in the other.

"What the bloody hell is going on here?" Julian demanded.

"He," Callie responded furiously, pointing an accusing finger at Brad, "intends to tear out Maudie's roses and plant lilies! And if Brutus doesn't rip his throat out, I will!"

Obediently Brutus lunged toward Brad, snarling and snapping. It took all of Julian's strength to restrain him. "Sit down and shut up!" he ordered sternly. To everyone's amazement, Brutus instantly obeyed. Julian turned a cold narrow gaze on his partner. "You're going to plant lilies in place of Maudie's roses? What are you, nuts?"

"Me nuts! Me? Forget it!" Brad shouted, backing away. "It's not worth it. I wouldn't buy this madhouse on a bet."

"Yeah? Well, who asked you?" Cory offered his two cents' worth.

"Shut up, Cory," Julian gritted, before turning to his partner. "Yeah? Well, who asked you, Brad?"

"What! Are you *all* crazy? You did! On the phone that day. But not now—you've blown it. You can keep your wormy bookcases and weird ceilings and all that disgusting wood. I'm getting a condo in the city." In two minutes flat, he was in his car and gone, only a swirl of dust left to mark his presence.

Julian turned to Callie. "Okay, I've played the tough guy. I've protected you, that mutt, and a bunch of silly flowers. Now will you tell me what the hell I was protecting you from? I assume I just broke up a very valuable partnership for a good reason. At least I hope it was a good reason. But knowing you, I tend to doubt it."

Cory glanced with interest from Julian to Callie.

"How can you stand there and ask me that?" Callie gasped.

"Uh-huh. Okay. I'll just phone him," Julian said, regaining his calm with surprising speed. "It takes three hours to get to Chicago—two, at the rate he's going."

She gasped in outrage. "You may have the right to sell Willow's End, but I'll tear the place down, piece by dry-rotted, de-walled, miswired piece, before I let you sell it to *him!*"

"That's plenty of time for him to cool off."

"He was going to put a *sauna* in the library."

"We could probably be back in business by this evening. Brad's not one to hold a grudge," he said confidently.

"Julian, will you *listen* to me?"

He sighed and dropped his hands to her shoulders. "I'm sorry, Callie. But you should have trusted me a little more. Even if I decided to sell Willow's End to Brad—which I haven't—I would have warned you first."

"But he said—"

"*He* said. *I* didn't say." He gave her shoulders a gentle shake. "I once did tell Brad that I'd sell him Willow's End. Don't look so hurt. It was said in a fit of anger, and I never meant him to take me seriously. I certainly never gave him any reason to think—once we'd learned the contents of Maudie's will—that I'd sell it to him. Or, for that matter, that I'd sell it at all."

She didn't dare hope. "You're keeping Willow's End?"

"Of course he's keeping Willow's End," Cory inserted. "Whatta ya think? He's nutty or something?"

"Thanks Cory," Julian said in a dry tone. "Was there something special you wanted, or did you come by just to try my patience?"

Cory thought for a moment. "The something-special choice. I wanted to thank Callie again for saving my hide. If she hadn't squared things with the cops, I'd be cooling my heels in the slammer this very minute."

Julian looked at Callie, his eyebrows raised in question. "That's what caused you to lose the bet? I'm surprised at you. The image of Cory in the slammer has a certain appeal. With Willow's End riding in the balance, you didn't have even a moment's hesitation?"

"Not a one," Callie stated firmly. She stepped into his arms, her hands tight about his neck. "And I'll tell you something else. You can sell the house, give it away, even burn it around our ears, and it won't change how I feel about you. You were right. Home *is* where the heart is, and both my home and my heart are right here—in your arms. I love you, Julian Lord. Now what do you have to say about that?''

Julian grinned. "Seems there's only one thing I can say."

"Which is?" she whispered.

He lowered his head, his mouth a mere breath away from hers. "That I love you. That I want to marry you. And that I want to live here with you and have children with you and raise them here, in Willow's End."

Tears filled her eyes. "You're willing to do that? Even though I failed you? Even though I lost the bet?"

Julian held her tight against him. "You didn't fail me. You'd never fail me. Do you think I'd put that stupid bet above something as important as our kids? All I ever wanted was for you to set a few priorities. You did that. I'm proud of you."

"But all that business about saying no..."

"Admit it, Callie. You do have trouble saying no. And you tend to take on more than you should. I just wanted you to learn to be more careful about which favors you're willing to grant."

"I think I've realized that." Her expression was troubled. "But I learned something else."

He smoothed her hair back from her face. "Which is?"

"That I like helping people. It makes me feel good. And I realized that you were right...about my mother." She made a little face. "She's one of the most selfish people I've ever known and I didn't want to be anything like her. So maybe as a result I overdo a little."

"Maybe a lot." Julian chuckled. "And don't worry. You're not the least like your mother." He dropped a kiss on her parted lips. "You're one of the kindest, most generous people it's ever been my privilege to know."

She offered him a brilliant smile. "I love you, Julian."

"I love you too, green eyes. And you're not the only one who's learned something from all this."

"No? What have you learned?"

"That despite my number-one rule, there are some things you'll do anything to keep, no matter what the cost."

Brutus thrust his nose between them, grinning expectantly from one to the other.

Julian's mouth brushed Callie's. "But I'm not sure your dog is one of them."

"Our dog," Callie corrected her ex-stepbrother, before she kissed him. "Our dog."

"Now this," announced Cory in a satisfied voice, "is what I call a happy ending."

EPILOGUE

IN THE EARLY HOURS of the morning, Julian awoke. His wife of less than a day lay curled up beside him, sound asleep. Her chestnut-brown hair spilled across her flushed cheeks and her arms were folded beneath her chin. For a long minute he simply lay there, watching her, amazed by the miracle of the love they shared.

If not for that love, he wasn't sure they'd have survived the wedding. Miller's Park would never be the same again. Images flashed through his mind: Callie, in a flowing white wedding gown, escorted down the "aisle" by Brutus; Brutus draining the three bowls of champagne punch and actually topping the infamous Founder's Day incident; Callie and Donna and Cory mugging for the cameras; the platters of sushi Brad had specially shipped in for the festivities.

He sighed in contentment. It was a day he'd never forget.

His stomach grumbled in hunger, and careful not to disturb Callie, Julian slid quietly from the bed and headed downstairs to the kitchen. Opening the refrigerator door, he pulled out a leftover platter of sushi. He stared at it for a long minute. *Give up,* he told himself. *If you're smart you'll learn to love it. Just like you've learned to love dogs who think they're people and ripped-apart houses and overly helpful wives.*

With a shrug of surrender, he carried the plate to the kitchen table and put it down beside a blank piece of paper and a pen. He stared at the pen thoughtfully, then picked it up. He began to write:

How to Survive a Happy Marriage
Chapter One: The First Year
Rule #1....

This August, don't miss an exclusive
two-in-one collection of earlier love stories

MAN
WITH A PAST

TRUE COLORS

by one of today's hottest
romance authors,

Now, two of Jayne Ann Krentz's most loved books are
available together in this special edition that new and
longtime fans will want to add to their bookshelves.

Let Jayne Ann Krentz capture your hearts with the love
stories, MAN WITH A PAST and TRUE COLORS.

And in October, watch for the second two-in-one
collection by Barbara Delinsky!

Available wherever Harlequin books are sold.

HARLEQUIN

Romance®

**This September, travel to England
with Harlequin Romance
FIRST CLASS title #3149,
ROSES HAVE THORNS
by Betty Neels**

It was Radolf Nauta's fault that Sarah lost her job at the hospital and was forced to look elsewhere for a living. So she wasn't particulary pleased to meet him again in a totally different environment. Not that he seemed disposed to be gracious to her: arrogant, opinionated and entirely too sure of himself, Radolf was just the sort of man Sarah disliked most. And yet, the more she saw of him, the more she found herself wondering what he really thought about her—which was stupid, because he was the last man on earth she could ever love....

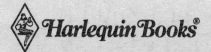 **Harlequin Books®**

GREAT NEWS...

HARLEQUIN UNVEILS NEW SHIPPING PLANS

For the convenience of customers, Harlequin has announced that Harlequin romances will now be available in stores at these convenient times each month*:

Harlequin Presents, American Romance, Historical, Intrigue:

> May titles: April 10
> June titles: May 8
> July titles: June 5
> August titles: July 10

Harlequin Romance, Superromance, Temptation, Regency Romance:

> May titles: April 24
> June titles: May 22
> July titles: June 19
> August titles: July 24

We hope this new schedule is convenient for you.

With only two trips each month to your local bookseller, you'll never miss any of your favorite authors!

*Please note: There may be slight variations in on-sale dates in your area due to differences in shipping and handling.

*Applicable to U.S. only.

Harlequin Superromance®

Available in Superromance this month
#462—STARLIT PROMISE

STARLIT PROMISE is a deeply moving story of a
woman coming to terms with her grief and gradually
opening her heart to life and love.

Author Petra Holland sets the scene beautifully, never
allowing her heroine to become mired in self-pity. It
is a story that will touch your heart and leave you
celebrating the strength of the human spirit.

**Available wherever Harlequin books
are sold.**

STARLIT-A